More praise for Deborah Adams and her Jesus Creek mysteries!

"This gentle, funny, suspenseful mystery series deserves a huge audience of devoted fans."
—NANCY PICKARD

"Deborah Adams brings the rustic wit and wisdom of Lake Wobegon to the plains of middle Tennessee."
—SHARYN MCCRUMB

"Ms. Adams captures both the intricacy and style of a well-crafted mystery, along with the comic elements of a truly Gothic Southern novel. In the process, she transcends both."
—STEVEN WOMACK

"Adams' books perfectly capture the rhythms of life in a small town, where everyone sees it as a God-given right to know everybody else's business."
—*The Baltimore Sun*

"Thoroughly enjoyable . . . A mystery novelist to be reckoned with."
—*Nashville Banner*

"In ALL THE HUNGRY MOTHERS, Deborah Adams brings her important message home: even in eccentric Jesus Creek, 'normal' is anything but, and crime is most horrifying when it's domestic."
—GILLIAN ROBERTS

Also by Deborah Adams
Published by Ballantine Books:

ALL THE GREAT PRETENDERS
ALL THE CRAZY WINTERS
ALL THE DARK DISGUISES

ALL THE HUNGRY MOTHERS

Deborah Adams

BALLANTINE BOOKS • NEW YORK

Copyright © 1994 by Deborah Adams

All rights reserved under International and Pan-American Copyright Conventions. Published in the United States of America by Ballantine Books, a division of Random House, Inc., New York, and simultaneously in Canada by Random House of Canada Limited, Toronto.

Library of Congress Catalog Card Number: 93-91027

ISBN 0-345-38552-7

Manufactured in the United States of America

First Edition: May 1994

10 9 8 7 6 5 4 3 2

This book is dedicated to the Women Are Safe volunteers.*

*Or maybe just to those volunteers who come to the meetings!

ACKNOWLEDGMENTS

We always see these list of names in books, people the author wishes to thank, etc. Most of us skip to the next page. But you really should read this one, because I'm going to explain how the following people have either helped me to write this book or have generally enhanced my life.

Diane Avril, the head honchess of Women Are Safe, gave me complete freedom to rummage through her files, and also assured me that she didn't expect me to become a volunteer, thus ensuring that guilt would force me to volunteer.

Karen B. Cecil provided one of my favorite lines of all time and proved that women can and do survive in the wild.

Holly Grady insisted on sharing gruesome stories about battered women and her theory about Jimmy Hoffa's final resting place. Suffice it to say, I'm glad I'm a vegetarian.

vii

Ellen Krieger provided another of my favorite lines of all time and taught me a valuable lesson in effective eavesdropping.

L. Bradley Law sent an amaryllis and a box of decapitated heads to cheer me up when I was down.

D. D. Maddox, who could teach Perry Mason a few things, taught me more about the legal system than I ever thought I'd want to know.

Charles May, bless his soul, saved my ego and my fax.

Rhoni McCollum and *Nancy Matthews* spent countless hours listening to me what-if, then backed me up and pointed out the errors in my reasoning. When I couldn't stand the pain of volunteerism (an incurable disease) any longer, Rhoni provided equestrian therapy. Now I hurt in new places.

Jean Newsome answered questions, and answered them well. I think it's fortunate that she's on the side of law and order or the world would have one formidable criminal to deal with.

Edie Rice-Sauer was gracious enough to provide information to a complete stranger. I hope in the future she will learn to be more cautious.

Terry West and *Megan Bladen-Blinkoff* suggested an addition to this and future books that is both useful and fun. Megan, you should have done this three books ago.

Dr. Cathryn Yarbrough lives with a mystery writer and therefore knows how to explain conditions such as psychological death in simple, easy-to-understand terms. And she makes one hell of a pesto sauce, too.

Ms. A through Z are the women who called (and continue to call) the domestic violence hotline seeking information, support, reassurance, or safety. They remind me that the truth cannot be repeated too often, and that anyone can be a victim.

CHARACTERS

I have received a few complaints about the number of characters in my books and the difficulty involved in remembering them all. As a Southerner, I have an innate ability to keep track of people and their relationships to one another. However, for the benefit of readers raised outside the South, I include here a list of characters in alphabetical order.

Janet Ayres: nanny and a newcomer to Jesus Creek

Delia Cannon: Jesus Creek native; former teacher; current library volunteer and amateur genealogist; divorced and occasionally living in sin with Roger for reasons no one understands as they are both too old for it to be sex

Jack and Charlie Daniels: two of the finest products ever turned out by the great state of Tennessee

Elvis: a legendary figure, appearing here and there, now and again, to this one and that one

James Forrest: Melinda's second husband and no better than her first

Katrina Forrest: Melinda's daughter

Melinda Forrest: a battered woman, often sheltered in the Leach home

Reb Gassler: Jesus Creek police chief; divorced from Marie, the town tramp

Tad Hopkins: a man whose only claim to fame is that he got drunk and stumbled across his friend's body

Oliver Host: an annoying, pretentious man who, though born and raised in Jesus Creek, affected a stilted, pseudo-British accent that causes regular folks to snicker to his face*

German Hunt: deputy police chief; not real bright, but he's a good old boy and his brother will always give you a sweet deal on a used car

Karen: a battered woman

Ariel Leach: infant daughter of Lindsay James and Sarah Elizabeth

Eliza Leach: mother of Lindsay James; daughter of William and Eliza Wilson; great-granddaughter of Captain John Wilson, retired and deceased, who served with distinction in Maney's Battery

Lindsay James Leach: husband to Sarah Elizabeth; son to Eliza; former editor of *The Jesus Creek Headlight,* the weekly newspaper that no longer exists due to unfortunate circumstances*

Sarah Elizabeth Leach: local librarian; wife of Lindsay James; daughter-in-law to Eliza

D. D. Maddox: Jesus Creek's answer to Perry Mason

Kay Martin's cat: Belladonna**

Missy and children: (last name withheld to protect anonymity); a battered family

Henry Mooten: fifth generation Jesus Creekian and it shows

Papaw: Janet Ayres's maternal grandfather; has never so much as visited Jesus Creek and is therefore of no interest to anyone in this story other than Janet

Frank Pate: owner of Pate's Hardware; once had a fling with a hula dancer while stationed in Hawaii during World War II and still brags about it

Puppy: unnamed canine deserted at a Dempsey Dumpster by some irresponsible jerk and later rescued by Sarah Elizabeth

Leesha Reed: Melinda Forrest's seventeen-year-old daughter from the first marriage, which ended in divorce as anyone could have told you it would

Pamela Satterfield: assistant librarian; the object of German Hunt's affection

Roger Shelton: a Yankee

Sam and Mina Tarlett: former residents of the Thorns' house; worked hard, raised their family, saved for the future, and never missed a Sunday at the Jesus Creek Baptist Church—you can't beat 'em

Eddie Thorn: Mary Ann and Ted's son; too young to have caused comment on his behavior or personality

Mary Ann Thorn: Sarah Elizabeth's new neighbor; another newcomer

Ted Thorn: Mary Ann's husband; known to be a hard worker, but still retains traces of a funny accent that causes many locals to distrust him on principle

The Tylers: former owner of a large, rambling, run-down house on the outskirts of town; they died some time back, but folks still speak of them with great affection

Constance Winter: probably an octogenarian, possibly a nonagenarian; either way, the town's most celebrated madwoman*

*See *All The Crazy Winters*
**See *All The Dark Disguises*

INFESTATION

CHAPTER

1

THERE WAS NO POSSIBILITY OF WALKING,
so Janet Ayres was forced to wait inside Proctor's
Gas Station until someone arrived to rescue her.
She stood near her suitcase, the better to ward off
potential luggage thieves, and watched a late-
summer storm blast miniature waves through the
station's deserted lot. Across the street a weak
neon sign blinked ELOISE'S DINER and Janet silently
cursed the twist of fate that had caused the Grey-
hound to deposit her only a few yards from food after a twelve-hour fast.

The town was a dismal sight in the gloom of
late-afternoon storm clouds. Janet supposed it
would improve once the sky cleared. She could see
potential in the maple-lined streets and well-
tended businesses along the main street. Sturdy
flower boxes dotted the sidewalk and held masses
of gold- and rust-colored chrysanthemums. It was,
Janet thought, a town with personality. She looked
forward to becoming acquainted with Jesus Creek,
Tennessee.

Her employer should have collected her ten minutes ago. Janet had introduced herself to Mrs. Leach in a lengthy telephone conversation and was certain she had given the correct time of her arrival. She mentally deducted points for Mrs. Leach's lack of punctuality. There was no time to dash through the storm to the diner, and Janet seriously doubted the quality of the food would be worth the trip anyway. Options exhausted, she sighed and continued her vigil.

Behind her the grizzled owner of the gas station sat watching an afternoon soap opera on a black-and-white TV, the reception fading in and out as the wind rose and fell. He'd introduced himself to Janet upon her arrival, but when she'd insisted on answering his questions with monosyllables, he'd soon given up on conversation.

Two other men were perched on either end of a faded and sagging couch, occasionally exchanging comments about the weather and "that mouthy Erica." Janet assumed they referred to one of the soap-opera characters, although she couldn't be sure. She did not monitor daytime drama, or approve of it.

The tan Buick that pulled up in front of the station looked sturdy enough to weather the storm, even if the woman driving it did not. Sarah Elizabeth Leach, drenched before she emerged from the car, sprinted inside and smiled apologetically at Janet.

"I'm so sorry," she began, "but I had to make an unexpected stop at the Dumpster. Someone dropped off the sweetest little puppy and I couldn't bear to leave it there in the rain. Poor thing must have been mistreated, too, because I had to chase it for ages before I could rescue it. It was absolutely terrified. Oh, dear. I should have brought an umbrella. Do you have one? Never mind. We'd probably get soaked anyway. Here, let me carry your suitcase and you just dash out there and hop into the car."

Before Janet could introduce herself, or even verify that this woman was indeed her employer, Sarah Elizabeth had darted back out into the storm and thrown the suitcase into the backseat. Seeing little choice but to go where all her worldly possessions went, Janet hurried to the car and scooted into the passenger seat. Once inside, she was met by the unmistakable sound of an unhappy infant.

"She's been fussy all day," Sarah Elizabeth explained. "All the chaos at the house, I expect. I'm so glad you got here when you did. Another day without help and I'd have lost my mind. She's scaring the heck out of the puppy, too." Before pulling out of the station's parking lot, Sarah Elizabeth leaned over the seat to inspect the damp and smelly animal that cowered in the floor.

"I'm Janet Ayres," Janet said, even though it seemed pointless to introduce herself now.

"Oh, good heavens. Well, I'm Sarah Elizabeth, and of course, that's Ariel in the backseat. I'd introduce you to the dog, but I haven't had time to think of a name for it yet. By the way, do you know how to tell if it's male or female?"

They had already reached an antebellum house just down the street from Proctor's Gas Station and Sarah Elizabeth pulled the massive car neatly into the driveway. "You go on up to the porch. It takes a while to get Ariel out of her safety seat, but I wouldn't dare go without it."

Janet nodded approvingly—she believed in child-safety seats, primarily because they trained the child early to sit still while inside a moving vehicle—and dared to hope that Sarah Elizabeth Leach would be a sensible mother. At Nanny Cares

Training Center, Janet had been warned about uncooperative parents.

Having arrived on the front porch, suitcase in
hand, she waited for Sarah Elizabeth. Coming from
a city of moderate population, Janet did not find it
odd that Sarah Elizabeth, baby in arm, had to dig
through her purse to find a key that would unlock
the front door. She could not have known that this
custom was all but unheard of in Jesus Creek.

Once the door was open, Sarah Elizabeth flung it
wide, struggling to hold on to the baby, the wrig-
gling puppy, and her purse while stepping back to
let Janet enter first. "Go on in," she said pleas-
antly. "Just drop your suitcase anywhere. Oh, is
that all you have? Or will more luggage arrive
later?"

"No," Janet assured her. "This is everything."

Sarah Elizabeth frowned slightly. "You can't
have much in there. Didn't you bring anything to
make yourself more at home here?"

Before Janet could explain that she chose to ad-
here to a life of simplicity, Ariel began to scream
again. "Let me have her," Janet said, taking the
baby before Sarah Elizabeth could refuse. She
threw Ariel over one shoulder and straightened
the receiving blanket that had gotten twisted
around the child's chubby knees. Then, flipping Ariel over, Janet wrapped the blanket tightly around
her, tucking in hands and feet, and clasped the
baby firmly to her chest. Ariel whimpered once and
hushed.

"Amazing," Sarah Elizabeth said with awe.
"Lord, am I *glad* you're here!"

The entry hall was spacious and would have been
bright and airy if not for the prematurely dark sky.
Directly in front of them was a staircase, the oak
banister polished to a high gloss. Tucked into the
space beside the stairs was a study table on which

rested a black touch-tone telephone, a large selection of pens and notepads, and several stacks of what appeared to Janet to be preprinted forms. The disarray clashed with the general orderliness of the foyer and disturbed Janet, who preferred organization in all things.

Through an open door to the right, Janet could see that the formal living room was equally spotless, and decorated with heavy dark furniture that had probably been in the family for generations. Her grandfather would no doubt have said the room appealed to her because her own ideas about morality and child rearing agreed with the old-fashioned view of the Victorians. Janet preferred to believe that she had a healthy appreciation for tradition.

She spied another small face peeking around the doorway on her left and for a moment was perplexed. "I understood," she said firmly, lest there be any misunderstanding about the gravity of this breach of agreement, "that you had only the one child."

"Oh, Katrina and her family are just visiting for a while. Aren't you, Katrina?" Sarah Elizabeth held up the soggy dog and the child came directly to her. "We have a new pet," she explained. "Katrina, this is Janet. She's going to live with us for a while and help take care of my little girl."

"Are you hiding, too?" Katrina asked.

"Let's go to the kitchen," Sarah Elizabeth said quickly. "I'll settle the pooch in the laundry room and then we can all sit down and chat."

With Ariel now half-asleep in her arms, Janet followed Sarah Elizabeth and Katrina to the back of the house, through the massive dining room and into the modernized kitchen. Hiding? she wondered. *Hiding?*

A small, drab woman in worn jeans and a man's oversized shirt stood at the kitchen sink, her back against the counter. Katrina seated herself at the table and smiled up at Janet. "Sarah Elizabeth, can I have ice cream?" the child asked.

"In just a second, Katrina. Melinda, this is Janet," Sarah Elizabeth said to the drab woman. "She'll be staying with us to help care for Ariel. I don't suppose we have dog food around here. Oh, well. I'll just give it food scraps for now." Sarah Elizabeth was vigorously drying the dog with an old dishtowel. "Why don't you fix Katrina's ice cream while I take care of the pup?"

Without a word, Melinda set about gathering bowls and spoons.

"There." Sarah Elizabeth put the puppy on the floor and watched it scamper to a dark corner of the kitchen, where it huddled in fear. "Poor baby. Melinda, if you'll just put a bowl of food down in the laundry room? Maybe the little nipper will calm down in a bit. And Janet, let me show you your room before I forget all about it."

Sarah Elizabeth motioned to Janet to follow her and together they retraced their steps to the front hall and up the massive staircase. "I'm sorry I didn't have time to warn you earlier," she whispered to Janet. "This is one of a number of safe houses in our county. We provide shelter to battered women, like Melinda. She and her children have been here a couple of weeks, but as you can see, Melinda is still stressed out."

"Her children? More than one?" Janet wanted to nail down the situation as quickly as possible, in order to ascertain her own duties.

"Yes, there's a teenage daughter. She's in school now, but she's such a quiet girl we hardly notice when she's around. Here, let me take Ariel off your hands and I'll put her in the crib." Sarah Elizabeth gently peeled the baby out of Janet's arms and disappeared into a bedroom to the left.

Janet followed, assuming that the nursery would also be her room for the time being. A Jenny Lind crib was wedged between the wall and a cedar poster bed, the latter being covered with books, clothing, and ladies' stockings. On the floor were several pairs of shoes, a purse, and a basket of clean but unironed skirts and blouses.

"Please excuse the mess," Sarah Elizabeth whispered. "I've been so busy lately I just never seem to have time to clean. Mother Eliza has a lady who comes in three times a week to do the rest of the house, but I can't stand the thought of someone nosing around in my private stuff." She covered the sleeping baby and motioned again for Janet to follow her. "Now, your room is just across the hall."

The room to which Janet was ushered was small, but not uncomfortably so. The window was dressed in pale blue curtains that had been pulled back to expose a second-story view of the neighborhood. Blue flowers dotted the wallpaper and matched perfectly the thick carpet on the floor. A bed, dresser, chair, and cherry writing desk completed the decor.

"There's a closet here that Mother Eliza had added last spring. And this door leads to a private bath, so you don't have to worry about standing in line." Sarah Elizabeth walked around the room, pointing out these things. "Unfortunately we don't have a phone jack in here, but you're always welcome to use any of the others in the house. Except after six P.M. on Friday nights. I have the hotline then, you see, and the line has to be kept free."

"The hotline?" Janet asked.

"The domestic violence hotline," Sarah Elizabeth explained. "Also, please don't answer if it rings on Friday night. Unless, of course, you'd be interested in becoming a volunteer, and God knows we could use you."

"I'll give it some thought," Janet said vaguely, hoping to deter further discussion of the subject.

Sarah Elizabeth did not seem ready to press it, for she quickly smiled and said, "I can't tell you what a relief it is to have you here. Not only to lend a hand with Ariel, but to talk to! It's going to be wonderful to have a normal adult in the house." She turned to leave, then added as an afterthought, "Oh, we leave for church at ten in the morning. You're welcome to join us if you like."

"Would you rather I keep Ariel here?"

Sarah Elizabeth shook her head. "Oh, no. I'll take Ariel with me. I always do. I just thought you might prefer another church or no church at all. Entirely up to you." She started out the door again.

"Mrs. Leach, please," Janet said, feeling that the time had definitely come to insert some structure into the proceedings. "I'll get my suitcase and unpack. Then we'll discuss the arrangements for Ariel, if that's convenient."

"Why, that's fine," Sarah Elizabeth said. "But for goodness' sake, call me Sarah Elizabeth. Mrs. Leach is my mother-in-law. Besides, we're not at all formal around here."

Janet had feared as much. She sighed resignedly as her employer left the room, then followed in order to rescue her suitcase and begin planning a program of attack against what most certainly would prove to be a difficult family.

It took only moments to hang her few skirts, blouses, and one good dress in the closet. Janet then set about arranging her books carefully on the desk—Emerson's *Essays*, a collection of poetry by Millay, a shabby but complete volume of Shakespeare, and, of course, the all-important Nanny

Cares *Training Manual*. When the time came, she would purchase a few superior children's books to read aloud to Ariel. Janet believed firmly in the importance of guiding a child's literary choices with care. Character was built on education, and education, of course, was built on one's introduction to fine literature.

Now that she'd actually arrived and was about to take her place in the Leach home, Janet allowed herself a momentary qualm. Despite her training and her high standing among the graduating class, Janet had no experience with children. Which was exactly the reason she'd chosen to become a nanny. Although still quite young, she realized that time was passing. To date she'd had no serious relationships, yet she expected one would come soon. And motherhood, upon which she certainly planned to embark someday, was not for the innocent. Janet knew only too well that mothers are made, not born. She did not intend to rush into the task without prior training, and what better way to prepare for parenting responsibilities than caring for a child?

Outside the storm continued, whistling around the corners of the Leach house like the soundtrack from a movie that Janet would never have paid to see. She glanced out the window, but because the storm had ushered in an early dusk, she was able to distinguish nothing more than the lights in the house next door. That one was certainly out of place, she thought. A modern brick split-level tucked into what should have been the Leaches' rose arbor. On second thought, perhaps it was the Leach house that was out of place. Nowhere else along the street had she seen antebellum dwellings.

Something about the house next door caught her eye and she pressed her face flat against the cool glass to determine what it was. She thought she could make out a face in an upstairs window. The gloom and pouring rain made it impossible to be sure, but it seemed to be the image of a waif, wide-eyed and pitiful, staring out into the dusk. Janet watched for a moment, trying to decide if it was an illusion. After a few minutes had passed without movement from the neighboring window, she decided that fatigue and hunger had made her too impressionable for her own good.

She took a moment to splash her face with cold water and comb her short, dark hair before descending the great staircase. She had considered the situation and determined to approach Mrs. Leach—Sarah Elizabeth, she reminded herself—in order that they might immediately and permanently decide upon a course of training for young Ariel. Katrina's laughter and the foul stench of what threatened to be dinner led her into the kitchen.

By this time the teenage daughter Sarah Elizabeth had mentioned was in from school. She was seated, along with her mother, sister, and Sarah Elizabeth, around the kitchen table as Katrina finished the last of her ice cream. The older girl, slight and nearly as drab as her mother, was intently underlining sections of a textbook and occasionally making notes.

"Janet," Sarah Elizabeth said brightly, "come sit with us. Melinda's making dinner tonight. White beans and a mess of turnip greens. I hope you're hungry."

Not any longer, Janet thought sourly. "Is this a good time to discuss policy?" she asked.

"Policy?"

"Yes. You've no doubt created a schedule for Ariel, which I'll certainly try to maintain. It occurs to me, however—"

"Oh, I don't worry much about schedules," Sarah Elizabeth said, flicking her hand to dismiss *that* nonsense. "Ariel lets me know what she wants and exactly when she wants it."

Melinda, head ducked slightly, nodded, as if she understood perfectly. Janet, on the other hand, did not understand at all how a parent could take so casual a stance about the upbringing of a child.

"Many experts feel that a strict schedule is important," she explained.

"Experts. Bah humbug."

The teenage daughter glanced up from her books, as if she might disagree, then changed her mind and returned to her studies.

"You'll have Ariel quite a bit of the time, I'm afraid," Sarah Elizabeth went on. "I work at the library weekdays, then have classes two evenings a week. Once in a while I have to work Saturday. But you'll always have Sunday off. You can count on that. Now, twice a month my mother-in-law and I will be in Memphis and naturally we take Ariel with us. Any other days that you need time off, just let me know so I can make arrangements for a sitter."

"Perhaps I'll draw up a timetable then," Janet suggested. "As for time off, Sundays will be sufficient."

Sarah Elizabeth didn't agree. "You'll go nuts if you don't get out once in a while. That's why so many new mothers suffer those miserable bouts of depression."

Janet felt the weight of disappointment settling upon her. She had so hoped that the Leaches would be a practical family. It seemed instead that Sarah Elizabeth, failing to recognize the necessity of routine and proper scheduling, would be the greatest burden in Janet's life. They had warned her about

this at Nanny Cares. Well, in due time she would
have young Ariel in hand, as well as the mother.

It did not please Janet to be forced into an evening spent before the television set. Nevertheless,
she joined the others in what could only be called a
rec room, thankfully tucked away behind the foyer,
where the mismatched furniture would not be seen
by casual visitors. Janet felt it imperative that she
spend a portion of the evening with Ariel in order
that they might become better acquainted. It would
do no harm, either, she felt, if she took advantage
of this opportunity to observe the members of this
unlikely household.

Unfortunately Sarah Elizabeth seemed determined to hold on to her daughter. In fact, it was
Melinda's teenager, Leesha, who monopolized the
new nanny, pulling Janet's life story from her in
bits and pieces.

"You've lived in San Francisco?"

"Briefly," Janet replied, "and many years ago."

"I've never been outside Tennessee," Leesha said
with a sigh of regret. "I'm even going to college in
Tennessee, to keep the tuition down."

This surprised Janet immensely. "You're going to
college?"

"Next year." Leesha nodded. "Maybe after that
I'll be able to travel."

The young woman was not at all what Janet had
expected. Throughout the evening, and despite the
distraction of television and conversation, Leesha
had applied herself diligently to homework, fight-
ing her mother's interference and constant urging
to "take a break, honey, before you ruin your eyes."
Leesha had shown herself to be a competent con-
versationalist (a trait she certainly hadn't inherited
from her mother), and her ability to retain and cor-
relate information was more than satisfactory.

"Have you chosen a career?" Janet asked, truly interested.

Before Leesha had an opportunity to answer, Katrina threw herself into her older sister's lap, demanding, "Flip me! Flip me!"

"There's not enough room in here, Katrina," Leesha protested.

Whereupon Katrina threw herself forward and tumbled into a table. Instead of crying from the damage caused by the impact, she picked herself up and cocked her head. "Lots of room!" she told Leesha. "Flip me!"

Melinda shook her head. "You're so rowdy, Katrina. You should have been a boy."

"Boys aren't necessarily rougher, Mom," Leesha pointed out.

Janet did not understand the sudden tension that crackled in the room. Sarah Elizabeth sat perfectly still, her eyes carefully focused on Ariel. Leesha seemed to be waiting for her mother to respond, but Melinda determinedly ignored the comment.

The uneasy quiet was broken by Katrina, who rolled her tiny hand into a fist and bounced it off Leesha's head. "Flip me or I'll *get* you," she promised.

CHAPTER

2

THE BABY WOKE BEFORE DAWN. JANET heard her crying and immediately rose from bed to attend to her duties. Wrapping a terrycloth robe around her simple cotton nightgown, she crossed the carpeted hall on tiptoe, hoping to get to Ariel before Sarah Elizabeth awoke.

"Hi, Janet." Sarah Elizabeth had already removed Ariel from the crib and was struggling with a fresh diaper.

"I'll be glad to do that," Janet offered, thinking that Sarah Elizabeth looked as if she could use the extra sleep.

"Nonsense. It's your day off."

"I've only been here a few hours. Certainly I have no plans for the day. And no doubt you could use the extra time to . . . do something." Janet had been going to say *to rest, because you look like hell*, but thought better of it. Nanny Cares had stressed the importance of refraining from personal comments. That sort of impropriety often ended in termination.

"Well, since you're already awake"—Sarah Elizabeth tossed the old diaper into a trash can across the room—"you could make the coffee. Strong, please. And I'll be down in a minute." She yawned.

After brushing her teeth and splashing her face with water, Janet descended the impressive staircase and entered the kitchen. From behind the laundry-room door came the whimpering of Sarah Elizabeth's puppy. Janet ignored its cries as she rummaged through the woefully chaotic cabinets in search of coffee, but once her mission was accomplished, it seemed silly to sit alone at the table while the puppy obviously longed for companionship.

"You foolish animal," she admonished when the dog ran from her and tried to wedge itself behind the washer. "You'll be stuck back there. Come here." Her no-nonsense tone had no effect and so it was necessary for Janet to drag the puppy out, then to hold it firmly in her arms to prevent escape. "What's the matter with you? Don't you realize you've been rescued? You have a home now, and Sarah Elizabeth will probably treat you like a"—she flipped the animal over—"queen," she finished.

The puppy was unimpressed and continued to whimper. "You're trembling. Silly baby. Iddy biddy fuzzy wuzzy. Is you tewwified?"

"Oh, good. You like animals." Sarah Elizabeth had entered the room so silently that Janet was caught without a reasonable explanation for her illogical behavior.

"She seems to be hungry. I'll put her back in the laundry room until you're ready to feed her." Janet did so, and quickly closed the door to prevent the animal's escape. If she ignored her momentary lapse, perhaps Sarah Elizabeth would, too.

The phone rang before that theory could be

tested. Sarah Elizabeth grabbed it, color draining from her face even before she said hello.

Janet removed Ariel from her mother's arms and settled into a chair, gently rocking the child to be sure she remained quiet throughout the phone conversation. From Sarah Elizabeth's expression and occasional comments, not to mention the fact that it was barely six A.M., Janet deduced that the call brought bad news.

She was correct. "I knew it would happen," Sarah Elizabeth said, after the call had ended. "Karen, one of our women, wound up in the hospital."

"Your women?"

"One of the battered women we've dealt with. In fact, she stayed here for a few days after her husband broke her arm. And then she went back to him." Sarah Elizabeth sighed.

"She's an idiot," Janet proclaimed.

Shaking her head, Sarah Elizabeth began to warm a bottle for her daughter. "Unfortunately it's a lot more complicated than that. In fact, these women return to their batterers an average of seven times."

"Seven times! It takes them that long to find a divorce lawyer?"

"Or to get killed. Or to kill their batterers." Sarah Elizabeth retrieved her child and offered her the warmed formula. "Maybe Karen will get out now. If she survives. They tell me she's in critical condition at this point."

"If only young women could be encouraged to complete their education! What can we expect when they are ignorant of the world and unable to care for themselves?"

"Karen's a lawyer," Sarah Elizabeth said quietly. "Well-educated and financially comfortable women are just as likely as anyone else to become victims of domestic violence. They're less likely to report it, though. Image to protect and all that."

There was no point in attempting a rational discussion, Janet realized. Sarah Elizabeth was the softhearted type (witness the stray animal currently housed in her laundry room) who would insist that these foolish women only needed care and guidance. Let a man even think about hitting me, Janet swore to herself, and he'll die swinging.

The coincidence of a determined pounding on the back door startled Janet in spite of her usually well-grounded nerves. Sarah Elizabeth bolted from her chair and thrust the feeding child at her nanny. "Stay here," she ordered, and hurried into the laundry room to peek through the curtained windows. "It's okay," she called. "Just Mary Ann."

Janet wondered who she'd expected it to be, and also why this Mary Ann felt it necessary to come beating on the door so early in the morning.

"This is Janet," Sarah Elizabeth said to the disheveled woman who followed her into the kitchen. "She's Ariel's nanny. Doesn't that sound uppity? And Mary Ann Thorn is our neighbor," Sarah Elizabeth explained.

Mary Ann Thorn was an attractive woman, or would be once she'd dressed and combed her thick black hair. The robe she wore over flannel pajamas was old and threadbare, but it revealed an appealing feminine figure. Janet was always pleased to find women who did not feel obligated to diet themselves to the size and shape of prepubescent girls.

"I'm awfully sorry," Mary Ann apologized by way of greeting. "Ted's going to be up in about five minutes and I'm completely out of coffee. I don't know why I didn't notice it last night and Ted can't live without his coffee. Could you spare a little?" She held out a plastic container like a beggar asking for coins, embarrassed by the action yet recognizing the absence of reasonable alternatives.

"Sure," Sarah Elizabeth said, and spooned Maxwell House into the Tupperware bowl. "We've already got some made. Do you want to join us?"

"Oh, no," Mary Ann said, heading out the door, precious coffee in hand. "I've got to get back. But thanks, and it was nice meeting you, Janet."

Given that Mary Ann hadn't even glanced in her direction, Janet doubted very much that it was nice. "Do you often have mornings like this?" Janet asked.

Sarah Elizabeth sighed. "Lately I have whole days like this. Whole weeks. Which is why I'm delighted you're here, even if I did hate the idea at first. My mother-in-law insisted we hire you, you see, although I think it had more to do with appearances than with concern about my stress level. I'm sorry you didn't get a chance to meet her earlier. She had one of her bad days and just kept to her room. But she'll be down in a bit, I expect." She poured coffee into two cups and handed one to Janet. "Mother Eliza lives in another century," she went on, "and believes the gentry must maintain certain standards."

So far, it seemed, Mother Eliza was the only member of the household to whom Janet could relate.

It was not until later that morning that Janet first met Eliza Wilson Leach. Janet had dressed the baby for church in a lacy blue gown, then repacked Sarah Elizabeth's diaper bag, making sure to include clean disposable diapers and removing two used bottles, a stuffed cat, a bag of crackers, and a week-old newspaper. Since Sarah Elizabeth was still dressing herself, Janet then took the baby downstairs and waited patiently in the living room.

The room met Janet's standards for both cleanliness and aesthetic appeal. Two tall windows were adorned by heavy blue draperies. The furniture that should have seemed slightly out of key with the house exuded a sense of stability and continuity. It was comforting to realize that one generation had built the house, another had furnished it, and still another kept it alive and moving steadily toward the future.

Sunshine streamed through the windows and granted her the first adequate glimpse of the neighborhood outside. "Look, Ariel. There seems to be a park just across the street. We'll be spending some time there. It's important for you to get fresh air. Later, of course, you'll be able to play there and perhaps we'll have picnics—"

"Ooh, picnics." Sarah Elizabeth sailed into the room, dressed in a pale blue shirtwaist that complemented her fair coloring. "I haven't had a picnic in years." She took Ariel into her arms and bounced her up and down. "Don't you look pretty?" she asked the child, as if expecting an answer.

Picking up the diaper bag from a nearby chair, Sarah Elizabeth turned to Janet. "Melinda and her girls are staying here this morning. They know the rules, of course, so I don't believe you'll have any trouble. But I do want to remind you not to open the door unless you know who's out there."

"Of course not," Janet said.

"Who is this one?" demanded a lean, dark figure from the doorway.

"Oh, Mother Eliza. This is Janet Ayres, the nanny. And obviously, Janet, this is my mother-in-law."

Eliza stepped closer to study Janet, then said with finality, "Doesn't look abused to me."

"No, Mother Eliza. Janet is the nanny. You remember. You insisted we hire one."

Ignoring Sarah Elizabeth, Eliza stepped closer still, took Janet's face in her hands, and turned it left, then right. "Who are your people, girl? You don't look familiar."

Stunned to silence, Janet looked to Sarah Elizabeth for help.

"She's from out of town, Mother Eliza. Come on now or we'll be late for church."

"Strangers in the house!" Eliza declared. "We'll have our throats cut in our sleep." With that pronouncement of doom, she started for the front door. "And don't forget little Lindsay."

"Yes, ma'am. I've got her," Sarah Elizabeth said, then whispered to Janet, "Don't mind her. She's a bit set in her ways."

Both women were gone before Janet could ascertain the identity of Lindsay.

Since there seemed to be nothing for her to do in the house, and since Janet did not relish the idea of sharing breakfast with Melinda and her daughters, she decided that Sunday morning was as suitable a time as any to explore Jesus Creek. Beginning with the small but tidy park across the street from the Leach home, she inspected the uninspiring statue and the enigmatic plaque proclaiming it a memorial to the heroes. Which heroes, it did not say.

Beyond the statue a woman performed an admirable Supta Vajrasana, sitting solidly on her knees, her body tilted backward until the crown of her head rested firmly on the grass. Knowing better than to disturb the serious practitioner, Janet started to move quietly away. But she was surprised to hear the woman call out to her.

"Hello? Who's that?"

"Janet Ayres," she replied politely. "Sorry to have bothered you."

"Not at all. Are you alone?"

"Yes, I am."

"Good. Help me out of this pose, please, before my legs go and I break something in the fall."

Janet hurried to the woman's aid, recognizing this as an aspiring adept who had gone too soon beyond the beginner's stage. Kneeling to give herself stability, Janet placed one hand under the woman's back and eased her body to the ground. It was a simple enough maneuver, especially for Janet, who had often assisted in such cases.

"Thanks! If Roger had come along and seen me, I'd never have heard the end of it." The woman raised herself to a sitting position and smiled. "Delia Cannon. You're Sarah Elizabeth's nanny, right?"

"I am," Janet agreed, rising and brushing grass and leaves from her knees. "A pleasure to meet you. In future, you might proceed more cautiously when attempting a new pose."

"Good advice. Getting into it was easy enough, but apparently I needed a different set of muscles to get out again. Are you into yoga?"

Janet shook her head. "No, but I've spent a great deal of time around . . . others who swear by its healthful benefits."

"Just as well," Delia said with a shrug. "You'll be too busy for much more than sleeping and chasing children. How's Eliza this morning?"

"Mrs. Leach is attending church with her daughter-in-law and grandchild. They all appeared to be in excellent health when last I saw them."

Delia eyed her closely for a minute. "You talk like Oliver Host. Well, I won't hold that against you. Hope you enjoy living in Jesus Creek." Standing up and stretching widely, Delia added, "I live right there, in the house that needs painting. Visit whenever you like. I'll be glad to explain things to you."

"What things?" Janet asked.

"You'll figure it out." With that parting riddle, Delia waved cheerily and strode off across the park and toward her home.

Janet watched her go, wondering if Delia Cannon would be safe on her own. The woman's eyes had been clear and bright, her manner certainly rational, but Janet felt that it was far too soon to draw conclusions about her state of mind.

Picking up a brisk stride (Janet believed in getting where she was going, even if that was nowhere in particular), she passed houses built in a variety of styles. Continuing along Primrose Lane, she recognized the diner and gas station from the day before, but there seemed little life in either of them. Across Main Street, however, on the courthouse lawn, there were two men playing checkers on a wooden bench. Janet had heard about small-town conviviality and felt obligated to attempt a cheerful greeting.

"Good morning, gentlemen," she said with false enthusiasm.

Both men looked up, obviously puzzled. "Where'd you come from?" one of them asked.

"Most recently I'm from the home of Sarah Elizabeth Leach," Janet answered.

"You one of them women she takes in? Reckon you ought to be out walking around?"

"Not at all," Janet replied haughtily, offended that anyone could mistake her for an abused woman. "I am employed to care for the child Ariel."

"Oh, well, that's okay then. I'm Henry Mooten and this here's Frank Pate."

Janet nodded to the quiet one and inspected the checkerboard. She had no idea how the game was played (Janet had never been one for mindless entertainment) and there seemed nothing else to say at that point.

Henry Mooten broke the ice. "Say you just come to town? Coulda picked a better time. Earthquake coming, you know." He lit a cigarette and inhaled calmly, as if this revelation had no more significance than an observation of cloudless weather.

"No, I didn't know," Janet said with surprise. "In fact, I wasn't aware that earthquakes could be predicted."

"Ah, that's what them experts tell you." Henry waved away the opinions of experts. "Royce Bartlett—don't guess you know him—he's a surveyor over in Benton Harbor. Anyway, he says down west of here a bit he can't keep his poles in the ground. It's just shiftin' ever' which way. Bound to get here before long."

Frank Pate gave her a wink and said, "Henry's keeping an eye on the ground for us. Don't want you to worry. He'll let us know when the big one's coming, so we'll all have plenty time to get out."

"Not the ground," Henry said peevishly. "It's the skies you gotta watch. When the aliens are finished up studying us, then they're gonna let loose with a rocket blast outta here and the earth's gonna go."

"Aliens." Janet felt certain that she now had a sufficient understanding of the situation. "Do you often see these aliens, Mr. Mooten?" Was there a professional in Jesus Creek capable of dealing with Mr. Mooten's problem, or would he have to travel to the nearest city?

"I ain't seen 'em at all. Could be they got some gizmo that makes 'em invisible. Or maybe they're just that way all the time. But I know for a fact they been here. Drive out toward the Tyler place sometime. They's a field out that way with one of them crop circles mashed down in it."

"Ah, Henry. That's just where the devil worshipers tramped it down," Frank assured him, as if devil-worshiping ceremonies were a far less formidable threat.

"I'll make every effort to do that, sir," Janet promised. "It's been a pleasure. I believe I'll be"—what was the vernacular?—"returning yonder," she finished. She was not unaware of the questioning look both men gave her as she retreated.

It took a mere ten minutes for Janet to complete her leisurely stroll through the heart of downtown Jesus Creek. She had specifically requested employment in a small town, hoping to absorb childcare advice from the motherly residents, age-old wisdom from the local sages, and a sense of family from the population at large. (The Nanny Cares ad had featured two cheerful career parents, two neat and glowing children, plus an obviously fulfilled nanny gathered near a roaring fire. BE PART OF A FAMILY, it had read. Janet had called the toll-free number immediately, recognizing a powerful inner need to be just that.)

And a small town this was. Definitely rural, possibly hospitable. However, she had not expected the high percentage of neurotic individuals. Perhaps she had met only the skewed ones first. No doubt she would get to know many stable and trustworthy souls in due time. She would make every effort to blend in here in Jesus Creek, to become one with her new neighbors and learn their ways.

Mary Ann met her on the sidewalk as Janet returned to the Leach house. "Hello, again," the woman called out. "I wanted to thank Sarah Elizabeth for bailing me out this morning. Could you give her this when she gets back from church?" Mary Ann held out a plate containing her token of appreciation. "I know she likes zucchini bread and she just doesn't have time to bake."

"I'm sure she'll be grateful," Janet said, taking the plate. "Oh, it's still warm."

"Well, I went straight home this morning and baked up a couple of loaves. I was going to leave it on the porch, but since you're right here, it would be better if you took it on in. Kay Martin's cat would get it otherwise."

"I'll be happy to do that, but you know there are people in the house who'd have been glad to accept this on Sarah Elizabeth's behalf," Janet pointed out.

"Oh, sure. But they don't really need to be opening the door to just anyone, do they? I don't understand how Sarah Elizabeth puts up with that, all those strangers roaming around in her house. Never any privacy." Mary Ann chuckled slightly. "Of course, I don't understand a lot of things in this town. Where I come from we have shelters, or at least a YWCA."

Hope flashed instantly in Janet. "You're new to Jesus Creek then?"

"Afraid so. We're from Louisville—our families are there and we've always lived there ourselves—but we moved down here because of my husband's job. He works over at Land. I'm used to moving fast and having places to go. That's sure not the way to get along down here." Mary Ann seemed wistful.

"Perhaps you can help me adjust," Janet suggested. "I've never lived in a small town either. It seems to me that ... well, that things are done differently."

"You mean they're all crazy here? Yeah, to me, too. I don't know if it's genetic or not, but there's something wrong with these people."

Shifting the warm plate to her other hand, Janet nodded. "I met a man this morning who believes UFOs are coming to destroy the earth."

"Henry? Oh, he's tame. Wait until you meet some of the real weirdos. I'm almost afraid to leave my house. I can't stand the thought of my children growing up here."

Ah, a mother. Mary Ann might be just the person Janet had hoped to encounter. "Tell me, how many children do you have?"

"Just one so far," Mary Ann said with obvious pride in her accomplishment. "Eddie is just two. We were thrilled to have a son first, of course, but I'd love to have a couple of little girls, too."

Janet nodded, recognizing the all-American male's dream—a son to carry on the family name. Parents were often consumed by the perceived importance of that label, while ignoring the other, more vital gifts that could be bestowed upon their offspring. "This is my first assignment within a family," she admitted. "I would be grateful if you'd allow me to call upon your experience from time to time."

Mary Ann was obviously flattered (as Janet could have predicted she would be) and patted Janet's arm reassuringly. "I'm sure you'll do a fine job. But, of course! Any time I can help you with that sweet little baby, you just let me know. Sometimes when I see Eddie growing so fast, I almost wish I could stop time. There's nothing like a baby in the house." Glancing at her watch, Mary Ann frowned. "I hadn't meant to take so long. Much as I'd like to talk some more, I'd better get back inside and get to work. We've been here six months and I'm still cleaning the previous owners' filth, plus trying to decorate. But you come over and visit just anytime."

"I'd like that," Janet said sincerely. "While I have been trained to care for children, I believe that experience counts for much. And although Ariel is still an infant, her social development cannot begin too soon. May I give you a call soon?"

Mary Ann nodded eagerly. "Please do. I'd love

the company." Looking around as if she expected someone else to be there, she added, "Sometimes I feel like I'm all alone here. Like I'm trapped and no one's noticed I'm gone."

Janet watched her new neighbor walk back across the lawn to her own house. It disturbed her that Mary Ann's cheerful personality did not match her rather morbid words. Why should the woman feel alone when she had a child, a husband, and neighbors all around?

Carrying the zucchini bread carefully, Janet ascended the wide steps that led to the Leach front porch. It was only then that she realized with dismay that she had no key to the Leach house. Feeling it entirely inappropriate to knock on the front door, she therefore walked regally through the still-damp morning grass and around to the back door that Mary Ann had used earlier. Melinda responded to her knock by peering cautiously through the curtained door.

"Oh, hi," Melinda said without emotion as she unlocked and opened the door.

"Zucchini bread from the neighbor." Janet held out the plate in explanation. "I believe Sarah Elizabeth is quite fond of it." She glanced quickly around, but saw no sign of the puppy, although the food Sarah Elizabeth had set out for it earlier was gone.

"Here, I'll take it. If I don't put it out of the way, my girls will have it eaten before you know what hit." Melinda placed the plate on top of the refrigerator. "I can make some coffee," she offered.

"No, please. It's too much trouble. Perhaps when the family returns. Do you happen to know," Janet asked, as an afterthought, "when they will return?"

"Should be about noon." Melinda sank into a

chair and shook her head. "I sure hope they're not late. I really need to talk."

It was not in Janet's nature to act as confidante, but Melinda's need was so obvious there seemed no polite way to avoid making the offer. "Would it help to talk to me?"

"Do you mind?" Melinda asked, with obvious relief. "I don't know what to do."

Janet seated herself in the next chair, recognizing the beginning of a long story. "What seems to be the problem?" she asked, hoping that it would be easily defined.

Melinda sighed before launching into her tale. "See, I've been here two weeks now. It's been so nice, too. Peaceful and all that. But James is just going crazy. See, I filed for divorce and all. And I guess he knew I meant business, 'cause I'd always told him when I left, it would be for good."

"James is your husband then?" Janet wanted to pin down the essential elements as clearly and quickly as possible. It might help to speed the account.

"Uh-huh. Well, he called my lawyer when he heard I'd filed and just begged to talk to me. 'Course he dudn' know where I am. But my lawyer passed it on to me. Anyways, I went ahead and called James, just, you know, to talk. Just to let him know I was serious. And he sure believes it. He practically begged me to come home."

"This was recently?"

Melinda nodded. "I've done talked to him two or three times and I called him again this morning. He sounds pitiful, you know? He swore it'd never happen again. So I'm thinking maybe, in a day or two, I might go back. But I've told him straight out, things'll be different."

"I believe you've done well to make that clear.

But, having made your decision, what problem is left to solve?"

Melinda sighed again. "Well, it's Leesha. You know, James is not her daddy. And they never did get along, either. I just don't know how she's gonna take it when I tell her we're going back."

"I see." Janet considered for a moment. "Has James abused Leesha or your younger daughter?"

"He's never laid a hand on either one of the girls, and he'd better not. But Leesha just can't seem to get along with him. I guess maybe it's that teenage rebellion. Still, I'd like for them to at least tolerate each other."

Janet, being of moderate temperament herself, failed to understand why Leesha's age should excuse her behavior. Recognizing, however, that she had never dealt with teenage children, she chose to withhold her advice on this subject. "If you have made your decision, then the best course of action, it seems to me, is to explain it thoroughly to your daughter and remain firm."

Melinda gave her a weak smile. "That's basically what James is always saying to me, too."

September 15, 1991

Dear Papaw,

I am comfortably settled in and have spent my first two days here getting to know the Leach family. Jesus Creek, by the way, is nowhere near Memphis. Thinking I might take advantage of a day off to visit Graceland (and only, you understand, on your behalf—I personally do not share your enthusiasm for that particular performer, nor do I know why you care about his personal life), I was informed that Memphis "would be over across the river. In West Tennessee." The tone implied that across the river is equivalent to across the galaxy, so I didn't ask for specific routes.

Ariel is two months old. She is a charming child, although her mother has failed to train her by providing a firm schedule. I believed that I will have her in hand soon. Unfortunately Ariel's family appears less than cooperative. The grandmother, the matriarch Mrs. Leach who lives here with us, is an odd character. Despite the fact that it is she who insisted upon a nanny, she has met me only briefly and then seemed more concerned with my ancestry than with my skills. The child's mother is high-strung and obviously a novice parent. She insists that I call her by her first and middle names—Sarah Elizabeth.

In addition, this area has no permanent shelter for the needy. Sarah Elizabeth has opened her home to complete strangers. At this very moment the Leach house contains refugees from domestic violence. I would suggest, if asked, that Jesus Creek is in greater need of psychological counseling services. My first encounter with the locals today made me aware of just how peculiar small towns can be. One is diligently observing the skies for signs of alien invaders and no one else seems to find this unusual.

Another practices yoga in the park, although not in the nude. (I have not yet recovered from that unfortunate incident in my youth, as I told you all along I would not.) Aside from being overly ambitious in her quest to master the art, she did not seem abnormal. Still one never knows.

The Leaches' neighbor, recently arrived here from a well-populated area, is no less confused than I by the behavior of Jesus Creekians. She theorizes a genetic flaw, no doubt complicated by generations of inbreeding. It is, of course, too soon to draw my own conclusions, as I have met so few of the locals, but I will not be surprised if her assessment turns out to be entirely accurate.

I feel that I have a lot to learn about the area, but expect I'll be able to make many useful contributions. Meanwhile I shall keep you informed of my progress with Ariel.

Love, Janet

P.S. Have you received a new address for Mother yet? I must admit I'm surprised that she left so suddenly and without informing us. I had thought that she was more than happy in the ashram.

The evening was clear and cooled by a slight autumn breeze that filtered through Janet's open window. Hers appeared to be the only room in the house so ventilated, and it had taken a mighty effort to get the window open in the first place. The rest of the household breathed dry, recirculated air, which Janet felt was not at all healthy.

She assumed that Melinda had discussed with her daughter the impending return to James. Leesha had been closed up in her room all afternoon and evening. Typical teenage response, Janet thought, and it should not be tolerated.

The rest of the Leach-home residents had taken after-dinner coffee on the broad front porch. While Janet gently rocked young Ariel to sleep, Sarah Elizabeth had struggled to study for an exam she would take on Monday. Melinda and her younger daughter, Katrina, chatted amiably at Mrs. Leach, who ignored them in favor of Janet.

"What did you say your name is?" the old lady

had asked. "Ayres? I knew an Ayres. Farm people. Would that be you?"

When Janet assured her that, no, her particular branch of the Ayres family had never farmed, Mrs. Leach seemed even less impressed. The old lady had then gone on to ask several pointed questions: Where are you from? How did you hear about this job? What kind of references can you provide?

Even though Janet had responded to each question, she had the definite impression that Mrs. Leach was dissatisfied with the answers. In fact, it seemed almost as if she hoped to catch Janet lying.

Now, leaning against the open window to catch a breath of night air, Janet felt a stirring in her chest. Were she a less hardy specimen, she might call it homesickness.

There was no light flickering in Mary Ann's window tonight. Probably the only house in town without a madwoman in the attic, Janet thought uncharitably.

The breeze carried a slight hum, as if a band of angry gnats might be headed her way. As Janet listened, caught in the mesmerizing rhythm of it, the sound grew and she was able to recognize it as human voices. Angry voices. Within seconds, the volume had increased enough that Janet could make out a few words. Nasty, vicious slurs thrown out into the night like weapons. And it was clear to her that the voices came from inside Mary Ann's house.

CHAPTER
3

JANET WOULD NOT HAVE ATTENDED THE
Thursday-night volunteer meeting if not for Sarah
Elizabeth's insistence on having Ariel present.

"I feel like I haven't seen my baby at all these
last few days. I'll just keep her with me. After all,
I'll only be sitting, for heaven's sake!"

It was immediately evident to Janet that this
would not be so. For one thing, the meeting was to
be held in Sarah Elizabeth's house. In addition, coffee and snacks were to be provided, which Sarah
Elizabeth would almost surely feel compelled to
dispense, thus leaving the child in the arms of each
and every volunteer present. By morning, the over-
abundance of attention and break in schedule
would have Ariel cranky and Sarah Elizabeth even
more determined to spoil the child.

And so Janet found herself sitting at the dining-
room table, determinedly clutching Ariel while a
half-dozen volunteers of SAN (Stop Abuse Now)
tried to pry the child from her arms. As predicted,
Sarah Elizabeth was the very picture of a good
hostess—serving food and drink, chatting superfi-

cially with every guest, and trying to reclaim her daughter in between.

Janet found it hard to believe that this small group of women handled domestic crises for four counties. "Hey," Sarah Elizabeth told her with mock pride, "we're taking care of a county that doesn't even offer us a volunteer."

The meeting began with updates on women who had recently moved out of safe houses, including the one called Karen. "She's doing a little better. The internal injuries weren't as severe as they'd feared. But she's not out of the woods, yet. The big problem is the sheriff—you know the one we've had so much trouble with before. Karen has an order of protection, but the police are lax about enforcing it. The husband has been to the hospital, which doesn't make Karen feel real good about her safety. One of the nurses happened to be in the room and knew enough to keep an eye on him."

"I suppose he apologized, swore he loves her, all that," one cynical volunteer put it.

"And brought flowers," she was told.

"Can we refer her to a shelter in another area?"

"Already have. As soon as she's released from the hospital, she'll go directly there. She's all for it this time. All it took was major injury to convince her he's dangerous."

The volunteers accepted this last with knowing smiles.

"Have you heard from Melinda since she left?" someone asked Sarah Elizabeth.

Janet had not been present when Melinda and her daughters left the Leach home, but had noted their absence with satisfaction. She felt strongly that the constant comings and goings of virtual strangers was not good for Ariel's sense of continuity.

Sarah Elizabeth threw the questioner a Look,

implying that it would have been extremely unlikely that she would have heard from Melinda.

"Well, maybe she'll be back soon," said the leader
of the volunteers, Pamela Satterfield.

At this, Janet could no longer contain her opinion. "I spoke to Melinda before she returned home,"
Janet said firmly. "She seemed quite pleased with
the prospect of continuing her marriage, and convinced of her husband's devotion and sincerity."

All the volunteers stopped chatting and chewing
to stare at her. Finally Sarah Elizabeth broke the
silence.

"Janet, hon, I guess I should have explained that
situation to you. See, Melinda's been with us three
times already, and every time, her husband talks
her into coming back. And every time," Sarah
Elizabeth continued grimly, "the abuse gets worse."

While Janet approved wholeheartedly of community service, it had occurred to her that the members of SAN might be verging on obsession with
their cause. "It doesn't seem reasonable," she
pointed out, "that he would abuse her again, knowing that she will leave him."

"Reasonable?" Pamela Satterfield's eyes bulged.
"Why isn't it reasonable? She's already proven that
he can beat her and she'll return. That he can
break her nose, and she'll return. That he can come
after her with a knife and drive her *and* her children into the street, and she'll return. He can do
anything he likes and she'll go right back."

Janet had no ready response. She had not known
that the attacks on Melinda had been this severe
and could not explain Melinda's willingness to return to such a life. "Does he drink?" she asked.
"Perhaps that explains—"

"That explains his behavior and the poor man
didn't really mean to do it and he's so sorry and

won't she please come back to him?" another of the
volunteers interrupted.

"That's what they all say," chanted the entire
group, then they broke into giggles.

"Sorry, Janet," Sarah Elizabeth said, refilling
coffee cups. "It's just that we've heard it all before."
The others nodded in agreement. "And ignore the
black humor you'll hear before the evening's over.
We're tacky, but it keeps us from grabbing our shot-
guns and killing these abusers ourselves."

Returning to the subject, Pamela Satterfield (an
efficient woman who had already earned Janet's
admiration) continued the earlier discussion. "How
did Leesha feel about this?"

Sarah Elizabeth shrugged. "She's just as upset
as always. I suggested that she stay here, but
Leesha feels she needs to be with her mother and
sister." Turning to Janet, she explained, "Last time
it was Leesha who got them out of the house.
Melinda wanted to stay until he sobered up. To be
sure he didn't hurt himself."

"Well, thank goodness he doesn't strike the children. At least he's decent enough to treat them
well," Janet said.

A silence surrounded her. "What?" she asked.

Sighing, Sarah Elizabeth went on. "We have no
proof that he abuses Leesha and Katrina. Nothing
we can turn over to the Department of Human Services. And the girls aren't talking. But sixty percent
of wife beaters also beat their children, so it's highly
unlikely that the girls have been left out of this."

"Oh, you needn't worry," Janet assured her. "I
asked Melinda myself, and she told me he's never
hit the girls."

Again, silence came from the group.

Friday morning had proved enjoyable. With
Melinda and her children evacuated, and Sarah

Elizabeth dashing off before Ariel awoke, Janet had found herself entirely in charge of the child's schedule. This, of course, simplified and enriched both her life and Ariel's. If only parents could see how well children behaved when left in the charge of a competent professional.

Janet allowed herself a moment of satisfaction as she dressed Ariel for an afternoon stroll. She had successfully completed a full week of employment and could already see signs of improvement in her charge. Ariel was sleeping well at night and had learned to nap without quite so much fuss.

Mary Ann had agreed by phone to join nanny and child for their afternoon walk, bringing along her own Eddie, and this pleased Janet immensely. She felt that it would be time well spent in many ways and looked forward to a guided tour of Jesus Creek.

She had not yet encountered Mr. Mooten's alien friends, although she was not at all sure that the entire town was not a species unknown to science. And if she did say so herself (which, of course, she did not—not aloud, at any rate), she was handling the elder Mrs. Leach quite well, in spite of that woman's probing and prying. The intrusive questions hardly bothered her at all now.

With Ariel properly attired, Janet donned comfortable shoes and set out, eager to spend time with the only Jesus Creek resident who spoke a recognizable language. Her schedule had been tight and this would be the first time she'd seen Mary Ann since overhearing the marital disagreement. Janet was understandably eager to avoid mention of it. After all, the argument had taken place in the privacy of Mary Ann's home and it was only by an unfortunate accident that Janet had overheard. No doubt many marriages suffered from bouts of temper, although Janet herself found this a poor excuse for engaging in verbal disputes. Calm voices and mature reasoning could always settle the issue.

She wheeled Ariel's stroller along the sidewalk, leaving it just below the three concrete steps that led to Mary Ann's front door. Tapping lightly on the door, she stood back a step so as not to seem overly eager. Mary Ann must have been waiting for her, for the door opened almost immediately and Janet saw that both Mary Ann and her son were ready for an outing.

"Hi, Ariel!" Mary Ann chirped, and snatched the little girl from her stroller. "Aren't you just adorable? Yes, you are. Yes, you are." Mary Ann showered Ariel with kisses, to the child's delight. "Babies are so precious." She sighed. "Come on in," she finally suggested. "We're almost ready to go. I have to finish cleaning the kitchen. Don't you just hate to leave the house undone? It's like the mess grows while you're gone."

Mary Ann carried Ariel into the kitchen, followed closely by a toddling Eddie. Janet brought up the rear, glancing around the immaculate living room on her way.

Mary Ann's house was a tribute to domesticity. White walls showed not a single finger smudge. The rose-tinted living-room carpet positively glistened and Janet could not help but notice that it had been meticulously vacuumed within the last few minutes. The furniture appeared to be nearly new, free of dents and dings and the normal signs of usage. Surely Mary Ann must be a leading candidate for housewife of the year.

The kitchen was even more amazing. It was carefully decorated in the traditional country style, and a duck motif was carried out everywhere. Ducks adorned the country-blue curtains. Duck wallpaper topped the chair rail, which defined an ivory paneling engraved with ducks in flight. A blue ceramic duck flowerpot served as a centerpiece on the small oak dinette table. More blue flowerpots with tole-painted ducks sat around the room, each one spilling forth healthy vines and plants.

Janet noted with satisfaction that the room and all its ducks had been scrupulously cleaned and polished. Mary Ann handed Ariel back to her nanny and busied herself at the kitchen sink, putting away recently washed and dried dishes.

"What a lovely home you have," Janet said, even though she felt as if she'd just walked into a fowl retreat.

"Well, someday it will be," Mary Ann said uncertainly. "I haven't gotten it clean yet. There's a smell in here that I can't get rid of. I've searched all over the house, even behind baseboards, but I can't find the source. Don't you think it smells like a dead mouse?"

Janet sniffed the air and detected only the slightly sweet odor of new paint and the scent of cinnamon potpourri simmering on Mary Ann's range. "I don't smell anything unusual," she said at last.

"Oh, you don't have to be polite. It's just awful and I know it. It seems to be down here somewhere." Mary Ann looked around as if expecting to find the reeking culprit in plain view. "Upstairs in my workroom I don't notice it at all."

"I hadn't realized you worked," Janet said with surprise. "What is it you do?"

Mary Ann laughed to dismiss the notion. "Not real work. I piddle with painting. I was working on an art degree when Ted and I got married. Just haven't gotten around to finishing up yet. I love watercolors, but I don't have much time for that. One of these days, though, I'm going to convert the attic room into a studio. Right now I just try to find a few minutes now and then to paint, so I haven't bothered to finish the room. Besides, I've got my hands full with the rest of the house."

Janet would have liked to see Mary Ann's paintings, but before she could ask for that honor, Mary Ann turned and announced that her cleaning was finished. "I'll just get Eddie out of the crib and we'll be on our way."

Stuffing Eddie into his jacket and hat, Mary Ann went on to say, "I'd thought we might run to Nashville later this week, but that's going to be a problem, after all. When I mentioned it to Ted, he reminded me that my car needs new tires before I take it too far from home. And he hasn't had time to check the oil and battery, he said. It's a good thing he knows cars, because I'd just drive it until it fell apart."

With little Eddie and Ariel strapped into their strollers, and Ariel wrapped warmly against the slight chill of a breeze, they headed out. This was Janet's first glimpse of the Thorn namesake and she discreetly sized him up, judging young Eddie to be of a pleasant temperament, if somewhat spoiled by his only-child status.

"I'm delighted that you could join me," she said sincerely as they set off down the sidewalk at a moderate pace. "I'd thought you might point out areas of interest in the town."

"There aren't any," Mary Ann said, straight-faced. "But at least you'll have an adult to talk to. A sane one, that is. I haven't noticed those girls in your backyard lately. Got the house to yourselves again?"

"The family Sarah Elizabeth was housing has moved out," Janet confirmed, trying not to reveal more than was necessary or prudent.

"Sarah Elizabeth is a real softie, isn't she? I admire her for opening up her house to people who need her help, but I don't understand how she can. You never know what sort of nuts you're getting. Of course, Sarah Elizabeth is probably used to anything. That mother-in-law of hers is a case and a half."

Since it would have been quite inappropriate to discuss Mrs. Leach's personality, Janet introduced a new topic. "What do the people of Jesus Creek do?" she asked. "Aside from watching for UFOs, I mean?"

Mary Ann chuckled. "You don't want to know. Seriously, there are all sorts here. You've got Henry, the alarmist. Eloise, over at the diner—she's a cross between Dolly Parton and a doting mother. Delia Cannon is the local activist. Out by the river there's a huge, spooky-looking place that everyone calls the Tyler house. Tylers don't live in it, but there you are. The people who do live there seem to be organizing a youth group of some sort. And some work over at Land Paper Company, like Ted. Then you've got your basic teachers and plumbers and what have you."

"I'm pleased to know all that. But I suppose I mean, what do they do for entertainment?" Janet couldn't imagine why she had asked, since she had always been able to entertain herself quite sufficiently. No doubt she'd asked the pointless question by way of making small talk until she'd gotten to know Mary Ann better.

"For entertainment they leave town. Are you kidding? What could they possibly do around here?" Mary Ann swept her arm through the air, as if presenting Jesus Creek in all its humorless glory.

"Yes, I see." There seemed nowhere else to go with that line of conversation.

"You'll have to find something to do with your time off, though," Mary Ann offered. "Sarah Elizabeth is always running around with one job or an-

other, so she won't be any help. And that old bat
Eliza probably thinks you ought to be chained to
the kitchen anyway. If you aren't careful, you'll go
nuts. It would be easy in this place."

"I'm sure I'll do fine. I must say, though, I'm delighted to have met you. No doubt we'll be able to
provide distraction for one another."

Mary Ann nodded her enthusiasm. "Absolutely.
I'd love it if we could run to Nashville one day,
maybe do some shopping. Sometimes I think if I
have to sit in that house another minute, I'll start
tearing my hair out. And I'm still trying to decorate
the house. I can't find anything in this town, but I
know some wonderful shops in Nashville."

"I'd enjoy that myself," Janet admitted. "I doubt
I'll be needing decorative items, but I am used to
having transportation of my own. In Jesus Creek,
walking suffices. Still, I'd enjoy getting away from
time to time."

"What did you do before you came here?" Mary
Ann asked. "How long have you been a nanny?"

"Ariel is my first charge," Janet said. "I grew up
in my grandparents' home and did most of the driving and shopping, as they never cared for those activities. And of course I tried a number of occu-
pations before settling on this one. It seems I'm a
late bloomer, having taken quite some time to decide what I want from life—" Janet stopped abruptly as the words registered in her mind. She
had the uncomfortable feeling that she'd just
sounded like her mother.

"Well, I know you'll love it," Mary Ann assured
her. "Children are the only reason for living. I don't
know what I did before I had Eddie. It seems like
the days must have been pointless back then. I
hope you won't wait too long to have your own children, Janet. Ariel is a doll, but you can't imagine
what it's like to hold your own child in your arms

and to know that *this* person is yours to love forever."

"Yes, well. I believe I shall first have to find a suitable man to marry."

"Oh, that's another story entirely," Mary Ann warned with a laugh. "Men are just like very large children who haven't been taught to behave. And by the time you get one, he's past redemption. You just have to put up with them and go on."

They had walked as far as the creek for which the town was named and cut across an alley to Morning Glory Way. A square brick building greeted them and a sign on the front proclaimed it the County Medical Center. It did not look sufficient to house more than a few patients at a time, and Janet doubted very much that the quality of care would inspire confidence in the seriously ill. She wondered if the battered Karen was being treated there.

"Hey, Janet!" a young voice called out.

Janet recognized Melinda and her daughters in the Medical-Center parking lot. It was obvious (to Janet at any rate) that Melinda was not overjoyed to see a familiar face, but Leesha had already started moving forward.

"Janet," she said, clearly delighted, "may I hold the baby?" Without waiting for permission, Leesha plucked Ariel from her stroller and began bouncing her in the air. "She's grown a foot in the last few days. Look, Mom. Hasn't she?"

Melinda stood cautiously by the car, a tentative smile on her face. She seemed content to let the conversation go on without her.

"I hope you're not ill," Janet said. It had occurred to her that there might be a far more disturbing reason for Melinda to visit the Medical Center, but it would have been rude to ask outright.

"Just a stomach flu," Melinda told her. "Leesha, don't drop the baby."

Katrina was less feisty than usual, but still managed sufficient spirit to tug on her mother's hand with enough force to pull Melinda off balance. "Gotta go," the little girl insisted. "Gotta go now."

"Relax, Mom." Leesha continued to bounce Ariel, seemingly delighted to be near the child. "How's Sarah Elizabeth? And the puppy?"

"Quite well, both of them," Janet assured her. "They've not yet named the animal, but it seems to be calming down nicely. I believe it actually came out into the open this morning when Sarah Elizabeth fed it."

"It's just awful the way people dump their pets like that." Leesha reluctantly returned Ariel to her stroller. "You'd think they'd have the decency to at least take them to the animal shelter, if nothing else."

"I couldn't agree more," Janet told her. "Irresponsibility is, I have no doubt, the primary cause of all that is amiss in the current world." Catching Leesha's eyes, she added, "But enough of that. Are you settling in at home?"

There was a distinct and uneasy pause before Leesha answered. "So far," she said quietly, her unwillingness to look at Janet a clear indication of the lie.

"Gotta go now," Katrina said more forcefully.

"We'd better get going," Melinda agreed. "Good to see you."

Leesha smiled a goodbye and got in behind the steering wheel. "Tell Sarah Elizabeth I'll come by for a visit sometime."

As the car pulled out of the parking lot and headed out of town, Mary Ann spoke for the first time. "Those are the people who've been staying with Sarah Elizabeth, aren't they? I recognized the girls." She shook her head. "I can't imagine why women put up with that. If Ted ever laid a hand on me, I'd be gone. No, I take that back. I'd kill him. Why should *I* leave home?"

"I find it hard to understand, too. Particularly when children are involved. As you can see, Leesha is quite a charming young woman. Capable and intelligent." Janet shook her head, in confusion and pity.

"We'd better finish our walk and get home. I left dinner in the oven and Ted's due any minute." Mary Ann turned Eddie's stroller and headed back up the sidewalk toward her house. "You'll have to meet Ted real soon. You'll love him. Everybody does."

They walked back up Morning Glory and around the curve to Primrose just in time to see a car pull into Mary Ann's driveway.

"Oh, damn. Ted's home already." Mary Ann increased speed and hurried to greet her husband. "Ted! Over here."

Ted emerged from the car and looked up in response to her voice. He flashed her a wide grin, then leaned back into the car to retrieve a parcel from the front seat. As Mary Ann and Janet approached he held it out to his wife. "I thought you'd like these," he said simply, handing the box to Mary Ann.

She gasped with obvious delight and removed the box top, then turned to show the contents to Janet.

"Roses! What a lovely expression of your affection." Janet smiled approvingly at Ted. "I'm Janet Ayres."

Ted gave her the same warm grin he'd earlier bestowed upon his wife and said, "Well, nice to meet you, Janet. I'm Ted, proud papa of this little quarterback." So saying, he lifted Eddie from his stroller and threw the child high into the air before catching him. Eddie seemed to accept this with calm delight.

"Ted, they're beautiful. Thank you, sweetheart." Mary Ann stood on tiptoe to plant a sloppy kiss on her husband's cheek. "I've got dinner going. It'll be ready by the time you've read the paper."

"Don't worry about dinner," he answered her. "I've got to leave again in a few minutes. I'm just going to change into fresh clothes and meet some of the guys for dinner. We're hoping we can get a ball team together. Play against the company teams from surrounding counties."

"Oh." Mary Ann was clearly disappointed, but said nothing. "Well, I guess I can save it for tomorrow night."

"So you're the nanny," Ted said, turning to Janet. "Mary Ann can teach you a few tricks. She's read every book there is on raising kids. To look at her, you wouldn't think she'd be the type, would you? It's a shame more women aren't interested in taking care of their own kids. But I guess then you'd be out of a job, wouldn't you, Janet?"

Something about Ted's comments rankled. Perhaps it was only his use of her first name, which seemed to her slightly more familiar than was proper on first meeting. Her grandfather, of course, would say she was being stuffy. Ted was still smiling and obviously had meant to be pleasant.

"I suppose you're right," she said. "And I'm certainly pleased to have been employed here and delighted that I am able to assist Ariel's family." Glancing at her watch as a convenient excuse for departure, she added, "It's been enjoyable visiting with you, Mary Ann. And a pleasure to meet you, Ted. I hope we'll have occasion to meet again. Now I must prepare Ariel for her mother's return. Good afternoon."

By the time Janet had reached the Leach porch

and carried Ariel, stroller and all, to the front door,
Mary Ann and Ted were entering their own home.
It was gratifying to see them, Janet thought. Arm
in arm, baby between them—*that* was a future she
envisioned for herself.

Sarah Elizabeth had taped notes to every telephone in the house, reminders of her hotline shift.
SAN used a diverter system, similar to the call-
forwarding option that Janet despised, to route in-
coming hotline calls to volunteers' homes. And even
though Sarah Elizabeth had earlier insisted that
this responsibility was no trouble at all, the phone
had been ringing steadily since she'd taken the hotline at six P.M.

Ariel, meanwhile, had developed a stuffy nose
and was whining intermittently. Janet was perfectly capable of tending a sick child, but Ariel
wanted only her mother and insisted on being cuddled nonstop throughout the evening.

"Where did you say you came from?" Eliza had
slipped soundlessly into the living room, where
Janet sat reading. "Excuse me?" Janet could not
understand the woman's obsession with ancestry
and besides, it was difficult to converse while
Sarah Elizabeth sat just outside, speaking firmly
into the hall phone and bouncing a crying Ariel on
her knee.

"I haven't seen your references. Where did Sarah
Elizabeth find you?"

Ah. This was a more proper inquiry and one that
Janet felt should have been made earlier. "I was
employed by Sarah Elizabeth through Nanny Cares
Training Center, one of the oldest and most
respected—"

"Nanny Cares? You may be sure that I will check
into this for myself." With that no-nonsense pronouncement, Eliza whirled around and out of the

room, presumably to return to her bubbling cal-
dron.

Would she actually contact Nanny Cares? Janet
wondered. Her stomach made a rapid U-turn before
settling heavily back into place.

"I realize you don't want to give up your job,"
Sarah Elizabeth was saying, "but if he kills you,
you won't have a job anyway."

Janet was sufficiently intrigued by this comment
to stoop to eavesdropping. There was silence while
Sarah Elizabeth listened to the reply, and then,
"It's possible that we could arrange transportation.
But if he knows where you work—"

More silence.

"You say you don't believe he'll hurt you. Yet he's
already tried to stab you with an ice pick."

Janet assumed that this caller was the same
traumatized woman who'd called twice before in
the past hour. The mention of the ice pick was a
dead giveaway. Sarah Elizabeth had been trying
unsuccessfully all evening to convince her that a
job was not as important as the continuation of her
life. It seemed the conversation was circling end-
lessly around the need to escape in order to continue living, but to work in order to afford escape.

Ariel's whimpering was growing stronger. Janet
could stand it no longer and marched boldly into
the hallway. There she plucked the baby from
Sarah Elizabeth's arms and carried her upstairs for
a warm bath. She had tried to be patient, tried to
fit into the routine (such as it was) of the household. But this family needed organizing, and if no
one else would do it, then the responsibility fell to
Janet. Ariel deserved at least that.

It took a half hour to bathe and dress Ariel. By
the time Janet had finished, Sarah Elizabeth was
sprawled across her bed, the SAN paperwork on
one side of her, a baby-blue Princess phone on the

other, and an open textbook in her hands. Sarah
Elizabeth did not seem to be studying so much as
dozing.

"I believe you'll sleep better if you clear the bed,
slip into a gown, and turn out the light," Janet rec-
ommended.

Sarah Elizabeth nodded in agreement, but said,
"I can't sleep until I finish this chapter." She waved
the textbook in the air. "I'd prefer to understand it,
but that may be asking too much."

"You can study tomorrow." Janet placed Ariel on
her stomach atop Sarah Elizabeth's bed while she
straightened the crib sheet and blanket. "It will do
you no good at all to exhaust yourself trying."

"Tomorrow I have to work. And Sunday we'll be
in Memphis. And the test is on Monday. So it's now
or never. And if it's never, I'll lose my job. Finishing
the degree is a condition of my employment."

Retrieving the baby, Janet put her into the crib,
covered her lightly, and began stroking her back
gently. This was one of the many useful techniques
for soothing fretful babies she'd been taught at
Nanny Cares. "If you lose your job, you'll have time
for Ariel and SAN."

"I know. And believe me, I've considered it! But
I don't think I'd last long as a stay-at-home mother,
especially with Ariel *and* Mother Eliza tugging at
me all the time." Sarah Elizabeth roused herself
from the bed and began to sort through the SAN
materials scattered about the room. "Sometimes I
wonder how the hell I got myself into this. I'm always too tired to continue the thought long enough
to find the answer, though."

"Obviously," Janet agreed. "I believe you are tan-
gled in the situation and therefore unable to view it
objectively. The solution is clear—you must give up
something."

Sarah Elizabeth stared at her for a moment, her

eyes filling with tears. "What will I give up?" she asked. "My life or my future?"

By ten o'clock the household had settled down sufficiently so that Janet could retire to her room. She sat by the open window, alternatively reading and looking out on the view below. The temperature had eased into the low fifties at night, giving crispness to the breeze that drifted through the screen. Absolute silence was not a sound Janet customarily heard, not at home anyway. It wasn't really silence, of course, but the lack of city sounds made it seem so.

Mary Ann's house was below her, sitting shrouded in the night mist. A single light burned in what Janet took to be the kitchen. She imagined Mary Ann and Ted, wrapped in cozy house robes, enjoying a moment of privacy over coffee while young Eddie slept peacefully in his crib. It was a scene that Janet had never experienced, of course—the romance of the long married. But she enjoyed the fantasy.

Without warning, Mary Ann's back door was suddenly thrown open and Mary Ann herself charged onto the concrete slab outside. Looking right and left as if hoping to surprise a visitor, she lingered, seemingly reluctant to admit that there was no one there. She continued to search the yard, behind the cars, and even behind the shrubs planted on either side of the door. Finally, having failed to find what she sought, Mary Ann went back into her house.

Janet watched as Mary Ann withdrew inside the door and continued to peer through the curtains at the empty yard.

OPPRESSION

CHAPTER

4

UPON ARISING, JANET NOTED FIRST THE glorious sunlight that streaked through her window. The top of a large maple that grew near the house, decorated with just a hint of dew and exposing its various autumn shades, was visible and glowing against a clear blue sky. In order to enjoy the beauty of it more fully, she pressed her face to the screen, expecting to bask in the morning warmth. Instead the sight that met her stopped her cold and set her heart racing.

Below the window, in Mary Ann's driveway, sat a Jesus Creek police car.

Wrapping her robe around her, Janet hastened across the hall, where Sarah Elizabeth was already dressing for the day.

"Something's wrong next door," she explained, completely forgetting the tone and manner appropriate to her situation.

"What?" Sarah Elizabeth looked up, clearly startled.

Janet realized then that a woman who spent her time among victims of violence *would* be startled, and chided herself for not handling the announcement in a calmer fashion. Instantly regaining her own composure, she explained. "There's a police car in the Thorns' driveway. I saw no occupant, nor did I see any of the Thorn family. There is no evidence of—"

Sarah Elizabeth was already on her way down the stairs, calling out to Janet, "Watch the baby!"

Pausing only long enough to change a diaper and wrap a heavy blanket around Ariel, Janet then proceeded to follow Sarah Elizabeth's example, even though she had not been asked to do so. She sprinted down the staircase and out the front door (left open by Sarah Elizabeth). Turning the corner of the Leach house, Janet could hear Sarah Elizabeth's insistent knocks on the Thorns' back door.

"Do you think we should intrude?" Janet asked, without any real thought of polite retreat.

"If they tell us to go away, we will," Sarah Elizabeth replied. "Otherwise I intend to find out what's going on."

The door was soon answered by a red-eyed Mary Ann. She, too, was still dressed in a house robe and slippers. Sniffing into a tissue, Mary Ann invited them in and motioned toward the kitchen table. There sat Ted, looking quite annoyed, and a tall, solid man in uniform. Despite sunlight filtering gently through lace curtains, and a host of cheerful ducks marching across the walls, the kitchen could not have been more laden with misery. Only little Eddie in his high chair, happily munching a piece of toast and playing knockdown with a sippy cup, seemed unaware of the palpable gloom.

"Reb?" Sarah Elizabeth began. "What's happened?"

The officer looked up. "Morning, Sarah E. Any trouble over at your place last night?"

Sarah Elizabeth shook her head hesitantly. "We don't have anyone staying with us right now."

Reb cast a suspicious glance in Janet's direction. "Oh, this is Janet. The nanny. Why do I always feel silly saying that?" Sarah Elizabeth shook her head at her foolishness. "Janet, this is Reb Gassler, our police chief. He doesn't bite, just looks like he does."

Janet nodded a greeting. "As Sarah Elizabeth has said, there are no strangers in her home at the moment. But in response to your question, we have had no time to discover whether there may have been trouble there. In fact, you've not yet explained the type of trouble we're discussing."

"My car." Mary Ann sniffed. "Someone destroyed it. The tires are slashed and wires are pulled loose under the hood."

"Y'all didn't hear anything last night, did you?" Reb turned to Sarah Elizabeth after only a quick, piercing glance at Janet.

"I didn't. I was out like a light as soon as I hit the bed. What about you, Janet? Your room's right next to Mary Ann's driveway."

Janet paused, wondering if she should mention that Mary Ann herself must have heard something, else why would she have been out prowling through the yard last night? "No, I'm afraid I heard nothing at all." She carefully avoided mentioning that she had *seen* something unusual. "When do you believe the damage occurred?"

"Not a clue," Ted said. "It's going to cost a fortune to get the car repaired. I don't know when we'll be able to afford it." He looked closely at Mary Ann, who seemed only vaguely aware of what was going on around her.

"Well, we'll check for prints," Reb said, rising from his chair. "Call your insurance company and see if they'll pay for any of it. And I'll let you know what turns up." He excused himself with a gracious goodbye to Sarah Elizabeth, a nod of the head to Janet, and a brisk wave to the Thorns.

"We've only got liability on my car," Mary Ann explained belatedly.

Ted rose, straightened his tie, and looked at his watch. "If I don't get to work, we won't even be able to afford that."

"Oh! You haven't had breakfast!" Mary Ann realized. "I'll fix something quick—"

"No time for that now. Guess you should have cooked before Reb got here." Ted threw a jacket over his arm and headed out the door. Within seconds they heard his car start and pull out onto the street.

"I'd better get Eddie's breakfast ready at least." Mary Ann flew into a manic rush, pulling pots and pans and breakfast food out of the cabinets. "You two want to eat with us?" Having fallen back into her mother mode, Mary Ann seemed calmer. Her sniffing had stopped and her voice no longer sounded like that of a whimpering child.

Sarah Elizabeth started toward Mary Ann, then thought better of it. "No, I'd better get Ariel home and set up for the day. I have to get to work myself. But you don't hesitate to call me at the library if you need anything today."

"And I shall be glad of your company if you wish to talk," Janet added, realizing that for all its sincerity, this did not sound like a warm and friendly offer.

"Thanks, gals," Mary Ann said to both Janet and Sarah Elizabeth. "I really do appreciate you coming over. But I can't think of a thing you can do." It was obvious that she had neither the time nor the desire to visit with them now.

"We'll talk later, then," Janet promised.

Mary Ann did not answer.

"I don't guess it was our business," Sarah Elizabeth said as the storm door closed behind them.

"No," Janet agreed. "Then again, we would not wish to ignore our neighbors in their time of need, using as a poor excuse our reluctance to become involved."

"There's a fine line there somewhere." Sarah Elizabeth sighed. "And I always feel like I'm on the wrong side of it."

Sarah Elizabeth held the front door of the Leach house open for Janet, continuing their conversation. "But they didn't seem thrilled by our concern. They *are* outsiders. As I recall, life is different in the real world."

Janet was still musing about the meaning of *that* as she stepped inside.

Eliza, fully dressed and neatly coiffed, met them in the hallway. "It's too chilly to have little Lindsay outside," she snarled at Janet.

"I've been meaning to ask." Janet turned to Sarah Elizabeth for clarification.

"The baby," Sarah Elizabeth whispered. To her mother-in-law she said, "Don't worry, Mother Eliza. We've kept her bundled up. Why don't you put the coffee on before I have to go to work?" Hustling the old lady into the kitchen, Sarah Elizabeth motioned for Janet to wait in the hallway. Once they were alone, she turned to the nanny to explain. "Mother Eliza was determined that the baby should be given a family name. Naturally she chose Lindsay Eliza. And she's stubborn about it, as you can tell. I just don't think a child should have to live up to someone else's name, do you? And I couldn't think of anyone I've ever met named Ariel, so that seemed safe enough. Except, of course, for that mermaid—"

"Not to mention the more literary association," Janet pointed out.

"Well, yes. But Shakespeare's freed spirit seems promising, if Ariel wants to live up to a namesake." Sarah Elizabeth shook her head and laughed. "Maybe I should have just dropped the Scrabble box and gone with the first handful of letters I picked up."

"I don't think so," Janet told her firmly.

The ringing telephone discouraged elaboration. While reaching for the receiver, Sarah Elizabeth turned to Janet. "Keep an eye on Mother Eliza, will you? Make sure she's put water in the coffeepot."

Almost as if she recognized the scenery, Ariel began to whimper for her breakfast as Janet carried her into the kitchen. A quick glance told Janet that the coffee was satisfactorily perking, so she shifted Ariel to one arm and cautiously opened the door to the laundry room. There was no sign of the puppy, but her food bowl was empty and wet paw prints leading from the water bowl to the back of the washer suggested that the animal was not dehydrated. Unfortunately, Janet noted, it was not housebroken, either.

She filled the empty bowl with dry puppy nuggets and vowed to return later to rid the room of its stench. A pity Sarah Elizabeth had chosen a housekeeper born (or so the woman claimed) with a paralyzing fear of furry creatures.

Having tended to one baby, Janet reached into the cabinets for Ariel's bowl and oat-flake cereal. There had been quite a bit of controversy at Nanny Cares about the diet of a child as young as Ariel. There were those who believed that solid food should not be fed to any child under the age of five months. Others proclaimed that nonsense. Janet, being unable to rely upon the good sense of family members for advice in the matter, had decided to follow the pattern already established by Sarah Elizabeth.

As she shifted Ariel to one arm while mixing cereal with her free hand, Janet was not unaware of Eliza's steady gaze upon her. There seemed a need for conversation, yet Janet could not imagine how to initiate it.

At last, Eliza shouldered the burden. "Sarah Elizabeth tells me," she began, "that you were hired through an agency with the unlikely name of Nanny Cares."

"Yes," Janet confirmed. "It's quite a respectable agency, in fact. I researched a number of training centers before I—"

"Located somewhere in the North, I believe."

"Why, yes. In—"

"And you trained there how long?" Eliza watched her without blinking.

"I completed the entire course. I hope it will not seem immodest of me to say that I graduated with honors." Janet suspected that it did, indeed, seem immodest, but she was beginning to feel the need to defend herself against Eliza's questioning.

"And what of your experience in caring for children?"

"Actually, this is my first placement. Mrs. Leach," Janet said, halting the motion of Ariel's cereal spoon. "Have you a complaint about my service? If so, I hope you will be direct with me." She threw back her shoulders and tilted her chin, thus affecting what she hoped was a confident, but not defiant, pose.

"We'll see," Eliza said enigmatically, and turned away as if Janet had ceased to exist.

Sarah Elizabeth entered the room just then like a minor tornado, moving in all directions at once, it seemed. "Janet, I've got to head out now. We'll be

getting a woman and two children in this afternoon
from a shelter in West Tennessee. I'll pick them up
at the bus station during my lunch break. In the
meantime, can I ask you to run to the grocery
store? Just get whatever you think we'll need for
dinner tonight and we'll worry about the rest later."

Eliza muttered something unintelligible but
clearly disapproving.

"Certainly," Janet said agreeably. "I'll be glad to
help. But may I ask why, if this woman is already
ensconced in a shelter, she now feels the need to
move in here?"

"Husband's a bloodhound," Sarah Elizabeth explained, gulping the coffee that evidently would
serve as her breakfast. "He's tracked her to three
different shelters already. We figure he'll never find
Jesus Creek. Just one of the advantages of a small
town."

There came a distinctly disapproving "hmmph"
from Eliza.

Sarah Elizabeth moved her coffee to the table
and sat down next to Janet. Taking Ariel into her
lap, Sarah Elizabeth finished dribbling cereal into
the child's mouth while making faces at her baby.

Despite her reservations about the possibility of
digestive problems occurring due to overstimula-
tion at mealtime, Janet remained silent on the subject. "Why is this man so eager to find a woman
who has surely made it abundantly clear that she
is ending their relationship?"

"He's probably one of those men. You know, the
ones who say, 'If I can't have you, no one will.' You
wouldn't believe how many of our women get hurt
or killed *after* they've left. Which is a damned good
reason to call the police, file a restraining order,
and generally cover yourself legally. But so many of
these women don't want to get their men in trou-

ble." Sarah Elizabeth shook her head at Ariel and told her, "Dey so silly, aren't dey? Yes, dey is."

Ariel seemed unimpressed and continued to hold her little mouth open for the next spoonful of cereal.

Sarah Elizabeth sighed. "I get that same look from abused women when I give them this speech."

Once Sarah Elizabeth had left for work and Eliza had retreated to her room (to boil a few bats' wings, Janet had no doubt), the house grew blissfully quiet. This allowed Janet and Ariel an opportunity to take advantage of the sunny living room and spend quality time discussing the headlines in *The Benton Harbor Sun*. It was, of course, a one-sided discourse, but Janet believed that intelligent conversation was important to the intellectual growth of children and that it could not begin too soon. Especially in this case.

They had just begun to cover the article about the latest school-board meeting when the phone rang. Janet took a moment to assure herself that it could not possibly be the domestic violence hotline before answering. She was surprised to hear a familiar voice.

"Um, is this Janet? I'm Leesha. I hope you remember me." The girl's voice was even more timid than Janet remembered.

"Of course, Leesha. What can I do for you?"

"Well, I was hoping I could talk to Sarah Elizabeth. If she's not busy or anything."

"I'm sorry, Leesha," Janet explained. "Sarah Elizabeth is attending classes this morning. I'd be happy to take a message."

There was a strained pause as Leesha considered this. At last she sighed heavily and said, "No, I guess not. I just wanted to tell her . . . well, I thought she might be able to help."

This sounded to Janet like an adolescent's plea for conversation. Taking a deep breath, and knowing she would regret it, she asked, "Perhaps I can help?"

"I don't know. It's the same old thing, really." Leesha sounded as if she were unsure of what problem she'd called to discuss. "Mom, you know. And him. I just wish she'd *do* something."

"Are your parents . . .?" What? Janet wondered. Are they arguing? Beating each other with golf clubs? How might one phrase this so as not to offend?

"He's starting again. I've tried to tell her it's gonna wind up the same old thing, but Mom just won't listen. She acts like she thinks it'll be different this time. And I've tried to tell her everything Sarah Elizabeth told her before. That it's just gonna get worse and all. She acts like none of it ever happened." Leesha's voice had taken on a tone of desperation.

Being inexperienced in such matters, Janet was reluctant to give out advice. Had she given advice, it might have been something like, *Give it up, kid. Your mother's nuts. Run like a rabbit and save yourself.* But no, that wouldn't do. "Why don't I have Sarah Elizabeth give you a call when she returns?" Janet suggested, thus relieving herself of all responsibility in the matter.

"No! She can't call. If he answers the phone, that'll make him furious. I'll . . . I'll call her at the library."

Before Janet could respond, the phone clicked in her ear. Replacing the receiver, Janet looked into Ariel's unconcerned face and whispered, "Your mother sure knows how to pick 'em."

The afternoon sun warmed Jesus Creek to near-summer temperatures and Janet thoroughly enjoyed her trip to the grocery. Ariel had been dressed in several layers of clothing so that, as the day grew warmer, the outer skins could be shed. Janet had also taken the precaution of attaching the stroller's visor so as not to expose the baby to potentially harmful ultraviolet rays. Janet's grandfather would have pointed out that children had been frolicking in the sun for centuries without undue damage, but then he didn't believe there was a hole in the ozone layer. Nor did he believe in the effectiveness of water filters or that regular physical checkups were necessary to good health.

Janet found Henry Mooten on the court square, happily making calculations on a drawing pad. The bench on which he sat was strewn with a number of interesting but surely unrelated items.

"Good day, Mr. Mooten," Janet greeted him. "I don't wish to pry, but may I ask what you have there?"

Henry held up his pad and proudly displayed a string of dates and times he'd written there. "I'm onto sumpin'. Look here. This here's a list of strange happenings I've heard about, goin' back three months."

Janet looked obediently, but simple dates didn't enlighten her. "What sort of happenings, Mr. Mooten?"

Henry flipped back a page and began to read. "First, we had five fires that all started for no cause. I got the dates of all them. There's three cases of fishing gear that just mysteriously disappeared. In the middle of the night." He said this last as if it might be significant. Leaning forward to play what he evidently felt would be a trump card, he whispered, "And all the power went out at the Video Arcade for ten minutes."

"Power outages are not that rare, are they?"

"*Only* in the Video Arcade," Henry stressed. "Just think about it for a while."

Janet was not sure she understood the point, but she felt that it would be neighborly to join in the game. "You know, a very strange event occurred just last night. Are you familiar with Ted and Mary Ann Thorn? They live next door to the Leach home."

"Ah," Henry said, "the new people. What happened over there?"

"Mrs. Thorn's car was vandalized last night. Is that the sort of unusual occurrence you're looking for?"

Apparently it was, for Henry began writing furiously on his drawing pad. Having made his notes, he turned back to Janet. "You see the connection? By golly, I've got it now."

His glee was almost contagious. Janet smiled brightly at the poor old man and wished him a good afternoon as she wheeled Ariel and the groceries on down Primrose Lane. Whatever his new hobby was, it was still better and healthier than watching for flying saucers, and Janet was delighted that she had been able to encourage him.

"Janet." Mary Ann came trotting across the yard to meet her, Eddie on one hip. "Would you mind if I came over for a while?"

"Not at all," Janet said truthfully. Ariel's lack of interest in world events was beginning to frustrate her. Adult company would be a welcome change. "I hope you're feeling calmer now."

Mary Ann shook her head. "No, not a bit. Janet, I don't know what's going on. The strangest things are happening, and at first I thought it was just me. But I've thought about this all morning. I've even made a list." She thrust a piece of paper at Janet. "Take a look. Tell me if I'm losing my mind or what?"

Janet scanned the paper. It was indeed a list, and it made no sense at all. "Noises. Lights on and off. Phone rings, no one there. Knocking." Glancing from the paper to Mary Ann, Janet waited for an explanation.

"These things keep happening. But only to me. Until now, that is. You can't deny that my tires were slashed." Mary Ann laughed nervously, almost as if she welcomed the vandalism as visible proof that she was not insane.

Realizing that Janet had no idea what she meant, Mary Ann continued. "For weeks now, I've been waking up at night. Hearing voices upstairs in my room."

"Ted doesn't hear these voices?" Janet recalled hearing voices emanating from Mary Ann's house, but chose not to mention it. Besides, she was fairly certain that was not what Mary Ann was talking about.

"No, he hasn't. He doesn't go up there—it's just a partial attic room, but I've been working on it. Fixing it up, you see, for myself. I wanted a place where I could go to read or paint or whatever I felt like doing. And just after I started cleaning it up, the voices started." Mary Ann pulled a Kleenex from her pocket and blew her nose. "Darned allergies," she muttered.

"What do these voices say?" Janet asked. She didn't suppose Mary Ann's answer would be of any importance. Clearly living in Jesus Creek had proved too much for the woman and there was nothing to be done about that.

Mary Ann readjusted Eddie, who'd been sliding steadily down her leg despite his death grip on her arm. "I don't know. I just hear them. I can't make out words. It's like a chorus of voices, calling to me. And when I go in to check, there's no one there. Of course."

"Lights on and off." Janet read the next item on the list. "All the lights? Or just in the attic?"

"Actually, it's a little worse than that. It's as if the whole house has suddenly gone dark. I can't see a thing—the first time, I thought I'd gone blind. And it only lasts a second, then everything's back to normal. I mentioned it to Ted once and he suggested I have my eyes checked. But there's more to it than just the darkness. I *feel* this darkness, like it's a huge wad of cotton wrapped around me."

"Ah," Janet said diplomatically.

"Last night I heard knocks at the door. I came downstairs from the bedroom and something— Janet, I know this sounds nuts, but something pulled me to the door. As if it wanted me to come outside."

"I believe I saw you," Janet confessed. "But there was no one there."

Mary Ann nodded. "I could barely force myself to go back inside. It was that powerful! And this morning, when I saw what had happened to the tires, it terrified me. Whatever it was, it was waiting for me. And when I didn't stay out there, it got angry and slashed the tires."

Mary Ann's problem was greater than Janet had first supposed. "Have you told all this to the police?" she asked.

"Are you kidding?"

Janet saw her point. "Well, then. Do you have any explanation for this yourself? Vandals? Someone who might be angry with you or Ted?"

"It's not Ted," Mary Ann said. "It's me. *My* car. No one else in my family is aware of any of this." Looking over her shoulder as if she thought they might be watched, she whispered, "It's that damned house. I think it's possessed."

CHAPTER

5

JANET HAD CONTROLLED HER TONGUE AND now wondered if that had been wise. If she would not advise Mary Ann to seek help, who would? This was Jesus Creek, after all, where paranoia, dementia, lunacy, and perhaps even lycanthropy were tolerated.

Still, if Mary Ann chose to believe that her house was haunted, did Janet have any right to disabuse her of the notion? Especially since Mary Ann seemed so excited by the prospect.

Sarah Elizabeth had attended morning classes at her university, then made the thirty-minute drive back to Jesus Creek and worked at the library all afternoon. During what should have been her lunch break, she'd picked up the latest houseguests, Missy and her two children, ferried them to the Leach home, given them a quick rundown of the rules, and left them in Janet's care to return to work.

Missy, a petite blonde, looked bright and capable—the way Janet supposed a promising young lawyer would look. Her children, toddlers though they were, spoke mature English and behaved themselves admirably. This did not appear to be a family living in terror.

Janet had attempted to make them feel welcome by chatting away about the town, about Ariel, about any subject that did not involve violence. Her efforts were rewarded by friendly smiles and intelligent questions about the town, which she could not answer, and about herself, which she chose not to answer. It was as if they were performers, Janet thought, acting happy, giving her what they thought *she* wanted from them.

Janet had worried that Missy's family would consume the time allotted for Ariel's afternoon entertainment (she was currently learning to listen patiently as Janet read a few of Shakespeare's lighter sonnets), but it seemed Missy had a schedule of her own. "We try to spend our afternoons reading and talking about our day," Missy informed her.

With the refugees tucked away in the rec room with much giggling and cheerful banter, and Eliza keeping to her own room, Janet found the afternoon far more pleasant than she had anticipated. Ariel had cooed softly throughout the daily sonnet and now slept soundly in her crib. Janet had turned on the monitor so that she could move about the house without fear of missing Ariel's waking cries.

She'd spent the better part of an hour scrubbing down the laundry room in a futile attempt to remove the dog smell. Once that chore was finished, Janet had turned her attention to the still-unnamed puppy, attempting to coax it out into the open with a chicken drumstick. Once or twice the little beastie had poked its damp nose toward the meat, but no amount of soft talk or nutritive enticement could convince it that the world was a safe place. At last

Janet left the chicken in the food bowl and admitted defeat.

Sarah Elizabeth, weighted down with paperwork accumulated during her frequent absences from work while attending classes, burst through the front door only moments before six o'clock. "Didn't think I'd make it," she said breathlessly, heading for the telephone in the kitchen. Punching up numbers to instruct the diverter to switch the hotline to the Leach phone, she began to shed clothes and shoes, stopping only to add another number to the series whenever she heard her cue. Then, jotting *Hotline* on a Post-It note, she stuck that to the kitchen phone and proceeded to do the same to every phone in the house.

"Just hope they give me time to pull myself together," she said to Janet when she passed her in the hallway. Pulling out her notebook and log sheet, Sarah Elizabeth set up her desk for action. "Do we have any coffee ready to go?"

Janet had already grown used to this ritual and had taken the liberty of preparing a full pot of coffee just before Sarah Elizabeth's arrival. She dutifully poured a cup and brought it to the living room, where Sarah Elizabeth usually stayed throughout her hotline evenings, that room being closest to the work phone.

"Bless your heart!" Sarah Elizabeth looked up from her textbooks and smiled. "If I can just get a quiet evening, maybe I'll be able to finish studying and still get some preparation done for the budget hearing."

"I'll be glad to help in any way I'm able," Janet said, knowing that her offer would be rejected. She seated herself in a green velvet wing chair, back straight and legs crossed demurely at the ankle. She wanted to appear ready for action, if action beckoned, while maintaining an aura of total confidence and relaxation.

"I wish. If you don't mind, just bring Ariel down when she's finished napping. I feel like I haven't seen her in ages." For a second it looked as if Sarah Elizabeth might cry, but she took a deep breath and regained her tough-old-soldier attitude. "How's Mother Eliza today? Still keeping to her room?"

"Yes. In fact, she hasn't come down since early this morning. I took the liberty of checking on her late this afternoon. She was not pleased by the intrusion, but I must confess I'd begun to worry that she'd become ill."

"Do you always talk like that?" Sarah Elizabeth asked with a giggle.

"Excuse me?"

"Sorry." The giggling continued, but Sarah Elizabeth tried to stifle it with her hand. "I'm punchy. Lord, I hope I don't get any calls tonight. The way I feel now, I'd probably tell some woman to get a gun and blow the so-and-so to kingdom come."

"May I suggest that you have a bite to eat and perhaps a rest before the phone rings, then?" Janet said solicitously. She had noticed that Sarah Elizabeth looked especially pale, and stress lines were clearly visible around her eyes.

"I'll grab a sandwich later. Delia Cannon was in the library today, doing more of her records keeping. She brought us a loaf of zucchini bread, so I'm not terribly hungry. Right now I just want to stretch out for a minute and pretend the world has gone away and left me in peace."

Sarah Elizabeth stretched herself full length upon the sofa and slowly rotated her head. Hating to interrupt the small moment of rest, Janet opted for a few moments of chitchat, but certain items would have to be dealt with before the day was done, or Janet herself would find it difficult to rest.

"I've met Ms. Cannon. I found her practicing yoga in the park across the street."

"Yep, that's Delia. She's been trying to get me to try yoga, too. She's into all sorts of weird stuff like that. I'd think she's the smartest person in town. Knows everything about the people here and the history. For the life of me, I don't know why she lives here."

"Perhaps she likes it here," Janet pointed out.

"How could she? Nobody else around here eats like her, dresses like her, thinks like her. Besides Roger, that is. And I'm not sure he agrees with anything she does. Could be it's a sex thing."

Janet chose not to pursue that. "Leesha called today," she said, when Sarah Elizabeth had resumed a sitting position and picked up her coffee.

"Yeah, she found me at work. She's the closest thing to an adult they've got in that family." Seeing Janet's mystified expression, Sarah Elizabeth elaborated. "There are cycles in abusive relationships. Anyone involved learns to recognize them soon enough. Leesha told me the tension is building—which means fists are gonna fly real soon. But Melinda refuses to discuss it, apparently in the hope that if she ignores it, it'll go away. Now, we've explained all this a number of times, but Leesha seems to have actually listened. She knows, even if her mother doesn't, that the battering is most likely going to get worse each time. The kid's scared half to death and with good reason."

"Surely a teenager's perspective—"

"I know. In a rational situation, it could be Leesha's imagination, or anger at her stepfather, or most anything. Trust me. Leesha has a good head on her shoulders. If she thinks trouble's brewing, she's more than likely right."

"Will Melinda return here, then? Before the violence begins?"

"The violence has already begun. Mentally, emotionally, the man is terrorizing the family. Don't discount the enormity of psychological warfare. And no, I doubt Melinda will get out before he beats her to a pulp. She never has before."

Janet sensed more than cynicism in Sarah Elizabeth's reply. She would almost call it indifference to Melinda's plight. Yet, if that were so—

"Did I sound heartless?" Sarah Elizabeth asked, apparently reading her mind. "Sorry. The first few times I dealt with these women, I was beside myself with anger and frustration. Now I just do what I can and make up tacky jokes about the rest."

This was not likely, in Janet's opinion. She believed, from her brief acquaintance with Sarah Elizabeth, that her employer was unlikely to make tacky jokes about women in distress. Still, she admitted, Sarah Elizabeth was proving more complex than one would have expected.

"Speaking of battered and deep-fried women, I looked in on Missy just now. Did you have any problem with her or the kids today?" Sarah Elizabeth sipped at her coffee. The caffeine appeared to relax her, improbable as that seemed.

"Not at all. In fact, they have been holed up in the rec room all day, enjoying themselves immensely, it seems. I suggested a nap for the children, but none of them seemed inclined to accept my advice."

"Can't say I blame them. The rec room is tucked away in the middle of the house. No exterior windows or doors. If you were running for your life, wouldn't you want to hide away, too?"

"This family seems so well adjusted. I would not have thought a woman running for her life could seem so pleasant and stable," Janet said honestly.

"Neither would I. But Missy's been at it for a while. I got a summary of her situation from the

Memphis shelter. She'd only been there three days when her husband turned up looking for her." Sarah Elizabeth shook her head.

"But isn't shelter information confidential? How could he possibly have found her there?"

"The police transported her to the Memphis shelter from the place she'd stayed before. Her husband evidently had one of his cop friends back home call *that* police station and ask for the information. Which is why she took a bus here. Hopefully the bus driver isn't her husband's old fishing buddy or anything."

"I can't believe the police would give out information of that sort!" Janet exclaimed.

"I know," Sarah Elizabeth said with a cynical smile. "I can't believe it either. Thank heaven Reb Gassler is better than the average cop. You wouldn't believe some of the idiotic stunts I've heard about in other towns. Over in Jameson County? They picked up a woman at a truck stop— she'd called the cops from there. Anyway, she told them her husband was after her and that she wanted to go to the women's shelter. So the cops took her in. Only they didn't bother to verify her story or even check her ID. And guess what? She turned out to be a wanted felon! Just looking for a free bed."

"Surely standard procedure would have impelled them to—"

"Standard procedure in a domestic violence case is to turn it over to someone else as quickly as possible. Like I said, Reb's smarter than that. And boy, are we glad to have him! By the way, did he dig up any information about Mary Ann's car?"

Janet shook her head. "Not to my knowledge." She replayed her earlier conversation with Mary Ann, wondering if any part of it had been intended as a particular confidence. "I hesitate to mention this, but surely, as Mary Ann's close friend, you ought to be informed."

"We're not *close* friends. Mary Ann is a reserved woman, and she's only lived here a few months." Sarah Elizabeth shot a look at Janet. "Please don't tell me Ted's beating her up. I can't deal with it right now."

Janet couldn't contain an amused chuckle. "Mercy, no. That's inconceivable. But I fear the problem may be equally disturbing. I wouldn't have you think I'm gossiping, you understand."

"Yes, yes." Sarah Elizabeth waved her hand, encouraging Janet to get on with the tale. "I promise I won't think you're gossiping. Tell me everything."

"Well," Janet said slowly, hoping to present the tale without resorting to sensationalism. "Mary Ann has recently taken notice of a number of experiences. I must say, I found this all quite subjective and couldn't—"

"Experiences," Sarah Elizabeth prodded. "What sort?"

"She has heard noises. Her telephone rings, but she finds no one on the other end. Most disturbing, in my view, is her insistence that the damage to her car, along with a number of other events, was caused by—supernatural forces."

"You mean she's bonkers," Sarah Elizabeth translated.

"Something like that. You know her better than I, and you have some experience in counseling. I thought you might—"

"Yeah, I'm a real help to the mentally unstable," Sarah Elizabeth declared, with only a touch of bitterness in her voice.

"Of course, if you feel she needs a professional, I could make that suggestion next time we speak."

Sarah Elizabeth took her time in answering. "If Mary Ann believes she's being stalked by ghosts, then I'd say she needs professional help. I doubt she'd appreciate being told so."

With that, Sarah Elizabeth rose to answer the ringing hotline.

Near midnight, Janet found herself gazing out her bedroom window while she gently rocked Ariel in her arms. The baby's crying hadn't even fazed Sarah Elizabeth, who had finally fallen asleep after a hectic evening.

Ariel had awakened just before dinner, cranky and stuffy-headed. Only Eliza would call these common childhood symptoms evidence of a terminal disease. Throughout dinner she had proceeded to berate both Sarah Elizabeth and Janet for exposing the baby to fresh air, irregular hours, and strange people. Missy had quickly registered the atmosphere created by Eliza and retreated with her children to their upstairs bedroom.

Having bored all of them with her tirade, Eliza had then switched to interrogation of Janet by way of Sarah Elizabeth.

"*Where* did you say you found her?"

Sarah Elizabeth was obviously embarrassed by her mother-in-law's behavior, but stopped short of pointing out that Janet was in the room. "I hired Janet through Nanny Cares, Mother Eliza. My sister's husband's sister hired her nanny there, as did three or four other people she knows. They've all been quite happy with the quality of care."

"No doubt. But little Lindsay is not any child. She has a heritage that requires particular nurturing."

"She certainly does," Sarah Elizabeth said, sounding ever so slightly snappish.

"And what references did you obtain for this . . . young woman?" Eliza sneered in Janet's direction.

"I told you, Mother Eliza. Nanny Cares sent me

a twelve-page questionnaire. They try very hard to match the nanny to the household. Frankly, I think they've done a wonderful job. I couldn't have asked for anyone to care for Ariel better than Janet does."

"You trust the opinion of total strangers? When it concerns your only child? I certainly would have been more rigorous in screening."

"No doubt you would have," Sarah Elizabeth said. "Unfortunately I haven't the time to spend entire days digging into Janet's background. I have a job, you'll remember, which *you* found for me. I also have classes, which I must pass if I want to keep that job. In addition, the weekends during which most women would be resting and spending time with their children, I am traveling back and forth to Memphis."

"Are you implying that my life was any less difficult?" Eliza demanded. "Do you think that because I restricted my activities to family—?"

"Not at all, Mother Eliza." Sarah Elizabeth was exhausted and ready to give up the battle. She rose from the kitchen table and took Ariel from Janet's arms. "I'm going upstairs for a while. I'll run the vaporizer and see if that helps Ariel to breathe. Once she's feeling better, I'll put her to bed." She made her retreat quickly, pausing only to whisper to Janet, "Run for your life."

Too late. Before Janet could move, Eliza had reached out and grabbed her arm. "Be aware that I keep an eye on you," she warned, giving Janet's arm a vicious shake.

Shortly afterward Janet had made her way upstairs. Across the hall from her room she could hear Sarah Elizabeth singing Ariel to sleep. It surprised her to hear Sarah Elizabeth's high, clear voice. One would not have expected that voice in a woman who looked as fragile as old lace. But if nothing else did, Sarah Elizabeth proved that appearances could deceive.

And now that Ariel was awake again, Janet was determined to avoid interrupting Sarah Elizabeth's well-earned rest. She swayed gently, humming under her breath and trying to soothe the baby. At the same time she watched the darkness below her window, thinking of Mary Ann.

Janet had never experienced anything remotely mysterious or mystical. She found it impossible, therefore, to understand why Mary Ann had immediately jumped to the conclusion that her house was haunted. Why, there could be any number of explanations for everything she had mentioned. If, as Sarah Elizabeth had warned, Mary Ann would not take well to a suggestion of counseling for herself, perhaps Janet could simply list logical explanations for each occurrence on Mary Ann's list. Getting her to see the sense of that might prove just as helpful.

Ariel having settled into a fitful doze, Janet decided to keep the baby in her own bed for the night. Not a practice to be encouraged, but the only way to ensure Sarah Elizabeth would not be disturbed. But as she turned away from the window something in the landscape caught her eye. The trees were swaying gently, graceful black dancers against the sky. A streetlight reflected off the top of Mary Ann's car lit up the area immediately below Janet's window, allowing her a better look at the shrubbery that surrounded the Leach property.

By laying the side of her face flat against the pane, Janet could make out quite clearly a human form darting from tree to tree across the back of Mary Ann's yard. She watched until it had disappeared behind the Leach house.

Adrenaline rushed through her, causing her face to flush and her entire body to tingle. Ought she to sound the alarm? But two deep breaths and good sense vetoed that idea. She would not disturb Sarah Elizabeth without good cause, and no one else in the house would be of use. Of course, there was always the possibility that Mary Ann had gone streaking through the night in pursuit of a ghost, but Janet was appalled by the idea of calling Ted Thorn to ask if he knew where his wife was.

In the end, she settled for a quick survey of all the doors and windows on the ground floor. Assured that locks were in place and in use, Janet returned to her room and spent the night rocking a wakeful Ariel.

A good night's sleep had done wonders for Sarah Elizabeth. She appeared at breakfast dressed in jeans and a sweater knitted from a becoming shade of rose yarn. "Pamela gave me this last Christmas," she explained, "but this is the first chance I've had to wear it. She makes the most wonderful sweaters, but I don't know where on earth she finds the time."

Janet, having gotten through the night on less than two hours' sleep, looked far more like a new mother than did Sarah Elizabeth. Her house robe had taken on the smell of soured formula, she needed a shower, and dark circles under her eyes added ten years to her appearance. Also she did not feel like making pleasant conversation. For this reason she hoped to have her breakfast and make a hasty retreat before any other members of the household could join them.

"I believe it would be best to keep Ariel upstairs today," she suggested to Sarah Elizabeth. "Although her head has cleared and she has slept quite well since five o'clock, an undisturbed period of rest would ensure continued good health."

"Oh, but we're going to Memphis today," Sarah Elizabeth reminded.

Janet was not entirely displeased to hear this. The absence of Ariel and family would provide an opportunity to sleep and thus restore her faculties to their normal sharpness.

"You look awful," Sarah Elizabeth commented casually. "It was nice of you to take Ariel through the night. It did me a world of good."

"My lack of sleep was not entirely due to Ariel's ill health," Janet confessed. "Near midnight I happened to glance out my window and I am quite certain that I saw a figure lurking about the yard."

Instantly she had Sarah Elizabeth's full attention. "A man? Where? Doing what?"

"I cannot say for certain that it was a male figure, but certainly human. I watched as it crossed from the Thorns' backyard into this one. Unfortunately I could only—"

"Why on earth didn't you wake me?" Sarah Elizabeth was already dialing the phone. "I'll have to get Reb out here," she said. "Wake Missy and tell her."

Only then did it occur to Janet that the mysterious shadow in the shrubbery might have been Missy's violent husband. The thought of it sent her scurrying to the guest room where Missy and her children slept, and caused her to knock a bit louder than she'd intended. Explaining the situation as briefly and quietly as possible, Janet then insisted that Missy dress herself and the children and stay put until the police chief had made his investigation.

This had taken only a few minutes, but by the time Janet came downstairs again, Sarah Elizabeth had not only contacted Reb Gassler, but was ushering him into the house.

"Janet saw someone in the yard last night,"

Sarah Elizabeth was explaining to him. "You understand that this could be extremely serious."

Reb nodded. "Could be. You had the house locked up, I hope?"

Sarah Elizabeth nodded absently. "We were going to Memphis today, but maybe I should stay here."

"Nonsense," Janet put in. "I shall be here. If there is even a hint of trouble, the telephone is but a step away."

Sarah Elizabeth seemed relieved that she did not have to make the decision herself.

"I'll look around the yard, see if there's anything there. Probably not, though." Reb helped himself to a cup of fresh coffee before settling into a kitchen chair. "First, though, I've got some more bad news for you."

Janet and Sarah Elizabeth gave him their full attention. Janet, at least, wondering if Henry Mooten was keeping track of all this.

"James Forrest was shot to death last night."

Janet remained perplexed until Sarah Elizabeth explained. "Melinda's husband," she said softly, not daring to ask Reb for more information.

"Mrs. Forrest checked into the Med Center around six o'clock and she was there all night. But time of death hasn't been established. We may have to bring her in." Reb reported the news without emotion, carefully avoiding Sarah Elizabeth's eyes.

"What about the kids?" Sarah Elizabeth asked. "Were they in the house?"

"They went to the hospital with their mother," Reb said. "That's all I've got for you right now. Mrs. Forrest seemed mighty upset about it all when she found out. Nurses said they had to sedate her." Reb finished his coffee in a gulp, set the cup on the table, and rose to go. "For the life of me, I can't understand why. Looks like she'd be glad he's dead."

"It's complicated," Sarah Elizabeth said, not bothering to attempt further explanation. "Thanks for coming by, Reb. If you find anything in the yard, let me know. You might want to check next door, too. Maybe they noticed something. For all we know, this man Janet saw could have been the same person who slashed Mary Ann's tires."

"I am not at all certain it was a man," Janet reminded them.

"Ah, Sarah Elizabeth just assumes it's a man," Reb said. "She blames everything on men."

Sarah Elizabeth gave him a friendly shoulder punch. "That's because you men are always causing trouble. Now get out there and get to work, unless you're waiting around for breakfast."

"No way," Reb told her, making his way out the back door. "Your mama-in-law might be here any minute. Talk about troublesome women."

Sarah Elizabeth diligently locked the door behind him and turned to face Janet. "Well, just another day in Jesus Creek," she said. "I hear Ariel. I'll get her dressed and fed while you take a shower. And if you want my advice, Janet, I think you should sleep some this morning. While you have the chance."

"Yes," Janet agreed. "I have a feeling I'm going to need my strength."

September 28

Dear Papaw,

In response to your query, no, I do not feel that I am stuffy. I cannot imagine why you would suggest that I "loosen up." Did I not spend three months living in a tent in Alaska? Am I not the only person you know who can build a one-match fire with wet wood? What more would you have me do? It seems to me that you should have grown weary of women prone to entertaining whimsy.

Having completed two weeks of service in the Leach household, I fear the battle will not be easily won. Sarah Elizabeth still maintains an informal attitude toward Ariel's upbringing. The elder Mrs. Leach, whom I'd hoped to enlist as an agent of discipline, has not warmed toward me. In fact, I have begun to suspect that she opens my mail and I have no doubt at all that she has, on at least one occasion, searched my room. Fortunately there is nothing she might have found that could cause embarrassment, but I do urge you to be discreet in your letters to me.

We are currently sheltering another displaced family. Sarah Elizabeth's devotion to her volunteer duty remains undiminished. She also continues to maintain a strict and exhausting schedule, which includes her work and school responsibilities, as well as social obligations. I regret to write that her frequent trips to Memphis are equally stressful for her. At last I have learned the story of those visits and I cannot express how much this concerns me. It seems that her husband, Lindsay James, is undergoing a form of medical treatment there, but that subject is best left for discussion at another time. Suffice it to say that Sarah Elizabeth, to her credit, remains cheerful and optimistic about his chances for recovery.

In addition, she has just this morning expressed her desire to obtain temporary guardianship of two children. You may remember that I mentioned a family, victims of domestic violence, who were staying with us when I first arrived here. This situation has grown tragically worse. The husband has been killed and the wife is hospitalized for treatment of injuries received just prior to his death. It is unclear at this time what

steps the police will take, but I fear the poor
woman will be interrogated unmercifully. I would
not say this to another soul, but I cannot help believing that she, in desperation and fear for her
life and the lives of her daughters, must have
killed him. Until she is released from the hospital, her children will be in Sarah Elizabeth's
care. I do not know what will become of them if
their mother is found guilty of murder.

Our neighbors, Ted and Mary Ann Thorn, are
having difficulties as well. A vicious attack upon
their car left it undrivable. As you might suppose, this has caused great anxiety in that family. I wonder if that could have contributed to
Mary Ann's vehement assertion that their house
is possessed by an evil spirit. I am at a loss and
cannot devise an argument that does not accuse
the poor woman of either deceit or mental insta-
bility. It might be best to humor her for the time
being. Do you remember the name of that exorcist with whom Mother was once employed? The
foul-smelling one, not the young one.

You may remember that I mentioned a Mr.
Mooten. He has recovered from his belief that
space aliens are lying in wait and now collects
unusual events. Given that he lives in Jesus
Creek, I believe he will be kept busy enough
chronicling these tales that he will have no time
for a relapse.

Speaking of Mother, I am glad that you have
enclosed her letter with your own. Please know
that you are welcome to read her letters to me in
the future, but I cannot urge you strongly
enough—*do not give her this address!* You may
not be surprised to learn that she is now affili-
ated with the Community of Pure Light and is
retraining her body and mind to work as one in
the spirit of purity. I gather this entails a regime

of meditation, fasting, and prayer to an unnamed deity. Also she has stopped eating anchovies, but does not say whether this is a spiritual sacrifice or merely a newly developed allergy.

I have discovered an interesting phenomenon on my daily walks through Jesus Creek. There is an inordinately high percentage of pickup trucks to cars in this area. Yesterday alone, I counted fourteen trucks in the parking lot of a local eatery, although fewer of them than I would have expected contained gun racks. Many of these vehicles seem to serve as mobile billboards, expressing the political, religious, and social affiliation of the owners by way of bumper-sticker art. For instance, just this morning I noticed one that instantly brought to mind my many discussions with you. It read: HONK IF YOU ARE ELVIS.

Without seeming to encourage your theory, I will go as far as to admit that, if Elvis lives, he probably does so in Jesus Creek.

All my love,

Janet

CHAPTER

6

JANET DID NOT GENERALLY APPROVE OF daytime naps for adults, so once she'd showered, dressed, and breakfasted, there was little left for her to do. The Leach family would not return until well into the evening. Missy and her children had been quickly relocated in the home of another of the volunteers, who, according to Sarah Elizabeth, had a horse farm so remote it could not even be reached by car. "I swear," she'd said to a disbelieving Janet, "the only time I ever ventured out that far, I had to park along the side of a dirt road, cross a creek on a two-by-four, and walk half a mile up-hill to the house."

Still undecided about how to talk sense into Mary Ann, Janet nevertheless chose to visit her neighbor and hoped that conversation would suggest an approach. Armed with good intentions, she tapped firmly on the Thorns' back door and readied a cheery greeting.

Mary Ann's appearance put swift end to any hope of bright morning banter. "Are you ill?" Janet was instantly alarmed. Mary Ann's eyes were red-

rimmed, her face puffy. The neck of her blouse did
not fully conceal raw scratches where her throat
seemed to have been clawed by the talons of some
frenzied beast.

Mary Ann stepped back into the kitchen and motioned Janet in. "Please come in," she said, almost
pleadingly. "I've got to talk to somebody." Dropping
into a chair as if all the energy had been drained
from her, Mary Ann then covered her face with her
hands and began to sob.

Janet was well aware that she was not a nurturing woman. Still she recognized the need for some
motherly action. Pulling a tissue from her skirt
pocket, she held it out to Mary Ann and attempted
a few soothing noises such as she might have used
to calm Ariel. None of this seemed to have any effect. It was obvious that more traditional comfort
would have to be offered. The choices seemed to be
brewing up a nice pot of tea or hugging.

"Why don't I make us some tea?" Janet suggested desperately.

"No." Mary Ann sniffed into the tissue and
seemed to be making a decent effort toward recovery. "I hate tea. Maybe some coffee. Just stick it in
the microwave."

Bustling about the kitchen, searching for cups
and then filling and heating them, Janet prayed for
guidance. She wondered if Sarah Elizabeth ever
felt this helpless when attempting to counsel her
hotline callers. Probably not. Sarah Elizabeth in-
stinctively and without resentment gave her all to
such matters.

With Mary Ann's emotional state slightly improved, Janet attempted conversation. "Ted and
Eddie . . . are they upstairs?"

Mary Ann shook her head violently. "Eddie's in
his playpen upstairs and Ted's meeting a friend for
breakfast. Just as well since I'm too upset to cook.

Janet, I'm scared to death. It's been bad enough already. Now the thing, the demon or whatever is haunting this house, has started to attack me!" She held open her blouse to expose more clearly the scratches there.

"When did this happen?" Janet asked, examining the marks. It looked exactly as if Mary Ann had attempted to rip open her throat with her fingernails. "And how?"

"I don't know. I woke up this morning and found this. It must have happened during the night."

"Mary Ann, are you sure you didn't scratch yourself while having a nightmare? Sometime—"

"I'd know if I scratched myself, wouldn't I?" Mary Ann demanded. "I'd have to be crazy to do this to myself. That's what Ted says, that I'm losing my mind. He doesn't hear the noises, he's never around when anything happens. Nobody is. Just me, and now I'm the one with the scars. Something is after *me*, Janet. And no one believes me."

This was clearly not the time to suggest counseling. Janet sat back in her chair and considered possible alternatives. It was only fair, she concluded, to give Mary Ann the benefit of the doubt. Suppose the house was truly haunted by an evil spirit. When her mother had worked (briefly, of course) as an apprentice exorcist, she had talked incessantly about the subject of possession. Unfortunately Janet had ignored most of her mother's babbling. She did, however, remember that demons were believed to lie dormant until an act of violence or invitation brought them into a home.

"Mary Ann, let's begin with the first incident. When did it happen, what was it? Be as specific as possible."

Mary Ann seemed surprised that Janet was taking her claims seriously, then almost embarrassingly grateful. "You believe me? Oh, thank God! I'm not crazy, am I?"

Reluctant to commit herself to an answer just yet, Janet forged ahead. "How soon after you moved in did unusual events begin to occur?"

"I don't know. At first there were a lot of little things that didn't mean much in themselves. It wasn't until I started looking back and adding them all up . . . you know. A phone call, but no one was on the other end. The sense that someone had gone through my purse or my closet, but nothing would be missing. Just annoyances, really."

"And this began when?" Janet was searching for a single event that might have set off a demon. Naturally she did not believe an unearthly force was responsible for Mary Ann's misery, but in locating a central event, she hoped to connect that to a rational explanation for everything that disturbed Mary Ann. She had had long years of practice ferreting out the significant information while her mother babbled on about astrological catastrophe, cosmic disruption, and assorted religious omens.

"I really can't say. Sometimes it feels as if it's gone on forever. But lately the sense of it has been . . . sinister. Threatening. The air in the house feels heavy." Mary Ann shook her head and sighed.

This was going nowhere, Janet decided. While she was trying to pin down dates and facts, Mary Ann simply wanted to talk about feelings of doom and gloom. For the moment she would leave behind the subject of threatening events and try instead a rear assault.

"What about the attic room? You said you'd heard voices there. Can I see it?"

"Oh, it's such a mess," Mary Ann protested.

"I understand that. But why not let me take a look? If we find nothing, we're no worse off."

Reluctantly Mary Ann rose to lead the way. A narrow doorway in the hall led to a flight of board steps. There was no light above the stairs, and only a single bulb, operated by a pull chain, at the top. The room was chilly and cramped. Even Janet, of medium height, had to stoop to avoid banging her head on the exposed rafters.

The floor was nothing more than sheets of plywood laid down across the beams. Here and there, insulation stuck out of the cracks. Most of the room was piled high with boxes of unused household items, but one corner had been cleared of those and now contained an artist's supplies—easel, paint box, a jar of brushes on the windowsill.

Glancing out the window, Janet realized that it faced her bedroom window across the driveway. This was the room in which she'd seen the mysterious light on her first night in Jesus Creek.

"You painted this?" Janet asked with surprise. She had spotted an incomplete, but beautifully done oil portrait of little Eddie.

"I don't often get a chance anymore," Mary Ann apologized. "I'd like to fix this room up as a studio, but the light isn't really good. And of course, there isn't much space. Ted says I should forget about it and just build on a room, but it might be years before we can afford that."

"Can't you paint in another part of the house?"

"Oh, I suppose I could. But you can see the kind of mess I'd have sitting around." Mary Ann swept her arm across the paraphernalia. "I wouldn't want this junk around. And I don't want to ruin the carpets, either. Which I surely would. Ted can tell you what a slob I am when I'm painting."

Discreetly peeking into open boxes and darkened corners, Janet found nothing to suggest that ghosts had been living there. "But you're sure the voices come from here?"

Mary Ann nodded. "Like they're calling me. Like they want me to come up here for something. I've looked and looked, but there's nothing here except my paint box. And these old unfinished pieces." She kicked gently at a pile of canvases leaning against the wall.

"There's no radio or tape player that might have been accidentally left on?"

"Nothing like that. I need absolute quiet when I paint. That's another reason I don't do much. With Ted and Eddie running around, how often can I expect peace and quiet?" Mary Ann laughed softly.

"Ted could take Eddie for a few hours, leaving you alone to paint."

"Oh, Ted's not very good with babies," Mary Ann explained. "Maybe when Eddie's older."

"Who owned this house before you moved in?" she asked. "Perhaps you should ask if they've experienced any abnormal events."

Mary Ann shook her head. "I don't know. Ted came down here when he was offered the job and bought the house then. I never met the previous owners."

"Surely you signed the deed!" Janet protested.

"Oh, no. Ted always takes care of business. It gives me a headache." She smiled at her inability to comprehend such complex matters. "I was never very good at that sort of thing. Home economics was my field, you know. I considered teaching it, in fact, but then Eddie was born just ten months after we got married."

Janet, having always been responsible for her own life and finances, was mystified. Still, Mary Ann's attitude was not unlike that of certain mothers who sprang instantly to mind. This of course did not mean that Janet could dismiss it easily, but educating Mary Ann was not a priority at the moment.

"Do you know Delia Cannon?" she asked. "I met her recently and Sarah Elizabeth tells me she is quite knowledgeable about Jesus Creek and its inhabitants. We can ask her about the history of your house." An idea seized her, one her grandfather would find reassuring. "In fact, let's drop in on her unexpectedly. I feel like being impulsive."

For Janet, it was a monumental stretch, but one she felt worth taking.

September was wrapping up the season in Jesus Creek. Maple trees along Primrose Lane and across the street in the small park were leaning toward their autumn colors. The nippy air and aroma of wood smoke from a not-too-distant fireplace reminded Janet of the comfortable, cozy life the Nanny Cares ad had promised her. They had neglected to mention violence, demon possession, sleepless nights, and she knew not what else. Someone, she thought, ought to teach a course in reality at that school.

The atmosphere of the town had changed as well. Although Janet had never seen the streets bustling, it seemed as if even the small amount of activity had slowed to a mellower pace. Was that possible? At any rate, it was a firm sense of settling in for winter that surrounded them as they strolled across the park to Delia's house on Morning Glory Way.

They found Delia sitting cross-legged on her front porch, dressed in jeans and a Whatsamattu U sweatshirt. She was contentedly sorting through a stack of dried flowers, separating them according to color and condition. "Hello, Mary Ann. Eddie looks sweet this morning. And Janet, right?"

"Correct," Janet assured her. "I hope we are not intruding."

" 'Course not. I was just looking for an excuse to

get off this porch. My backside's half-frozen. Want coffee? I've stocked up on vanilla nut."

"That sounds lovely," Janet said, although in truth she'd already had enough coffee in the last two weeks to fulfill her caffeine requirement for years to come. "Actually, we'd like information, too, if you don't mind."

"Mind? I positively love telling all I know."

Following Delia and Mary Ann through Delia's small house, Janet was amazed at the number of books, paper, and loose pencils strewn about the living room. "Excuse the mess," Delia apologized. "If you think it's bad, just imagine how I feel trying to live in it. A few months ago I finished alphabetizing the census records. Now I'm doing the same thing to marriage records. I must have been mad when I came up with that one."

Thankfully Delia's kitchen table was relatively free of clutter, so that they were able to relax there while the coffee brewed. Mary Ann jiggled Eddie on her knee while he amused himself by spinning Delia's saltshaker on the tabletop. Ignoring this, as did the child's mother, Delia asked, "I guess Sarah Elizabeth has gone to Memphis today?"

"Yes, along with Mrs. Leach and the child. I expect them back later this evening."

"Sarah Elizabeth is going to drop from exhaustion one day. Ordinarily Eliza is full of baloney, but her idea to hire you was a good one."

"I agree with you that Sarah Elizabeth needs someone to assist with her domestic duties. Mrs. Leach, however, does not seem entirely satisfied with the arrangement."

Delia patted her shoulder. "Don't worry about that. Eliza doesn't like anything. Never has. That's about half of what's wrong with her son."

Once the coffee had been poured and served, Janet felt enough pleasant banter had passed, and since Mary Ann seemed disinclined to introduce the pertinent subject, she did so herself. "Delia, perhaps you can tell us something about the previous owners of Mary Ann's house."

"The Tarletts? Sure. What would you like to know?"

"What sort of people were they? What were their interests? What was your opinion of them?" Janet was unsure what she expected to learn from any of this, since she most certainly did not believe that the Tarletts' satanic soirees had brought about Mary Ann's current troubles. Still, one had to begin an investigation somewhere and it would not do at all to have Mary Ann think that her delusions were being carelessly dismissed. Janet would present to her friend a clear and logical trail to follow, and together, perhaps, they would discover that what seemed now like supernatural mischief was in fact nothing more than creaky pipes, wind in the trees, and spicy food eaten too late at night.

"Well, for one thing," Delia began, "they were both about two hundred years old. Sam and Mina Tarlett lived out in the boonies all their lives and kept a fine garden, I might add, until about ten years ago when they decided they were too old for that life. So they moved to town—to Mary Ann's house—and had their first telephone installed. Mina never did learn to use it, but that's beside the point."

"Where are they now?" Mary Ann asked, her voice practically trembling. She seemed to believe that both Tarletts, or their ghostly spirits at least, might still reside in her attic.

"Oh, they're off at the nursing home. Moved in there when Mina got up one morning and declared she'd cooked her last meal. I always admired her for that. Someday I'm going to do it myself. Well, actually, I don't cook that much now. But anyway,

Sam agreed. Said he'd cut enough grass to last him
into the hereafter. They put the house on the mar-
ket, a few weeks later you folks bought it, and
that's that."

"So there was nothing unusual about them?"
Mary Ann was clearly disappointed.

"Not by Jesus Creek standards," Delia said.
"Why? What's going on?"

Mary Ann looked at Janet, who looked back at
her. Neither woman was immediately willing to explain. Delia, however, had learned much from her
years as a teacher and knew how to wait it out. At
last the silence became so uncomfortable that Mary
Ann was forced to speak.

"I think the house is haunted," she said simply.
"Call me crazy. I can't help it. That's the way it is."

Delia seemed more interested than skeptical,
however. "Really? I'd never have thought of that.
The Tyler house, maybe. Or—oh, dear. Henry
Mooten didn't tell you any wild stories, did he?"

Mary Ann shook her head. "No, I'm not talking
about UFOs. And I haven't even seen ghosts or
anything as definite as that. It's harder to explain.
Noises, odors, a feeling that the house is closing in
around me."

Janet watched Delia for her reaction. Despite appearances, she suspected that Delia Cannon was a
sensible woman who would weigh the evidence,
give it due consideration, and find a plausible explanation, all without ridiculing Mary Ann's fears.

"I have a book about that," Delia said suddenly.
"Wait here. I'll try to find it."

With Delia momentarily absent, Janet turned to
Mary Ann and said quietly, "You see. None of us is
calling you crazy. Clearly something out of the ordinary is happening to you, for whatever reason. A
cool head and rational action will clear this up in
no time."

Mary Ann gave her a grateful, if somewhat tentative, smile. "Thanks. I feel better just knowing someone is taking me seriously. If I disappear into a black fog one night, you'll know what happened to me."

"Good heavens! Why should you do that?" Janet suddenly feared that Mary Ann's delusions were worse than she'd expected.

"Because that's how I feel sometimes. Like I'm going to be swallowed up, sucked into another dimension or universe or whatever, and no one will even notice I'm gone or know where to start looking. I think my greatest fear is not that I'll die, but that I'll just stop being there one day."

"Found it!" Delia announced triumphantly. "*Demons in Our Day*. It's a 'sociological study of the spiritual elements involved in modern methods of exorcism,'" she read from the back cover of the book in her hand. "As I recall, it covers the subject of hauntings in a general way, focusing more on the spirits or demons that inhabit a building."

Janet did not ask why Delia had such a book. She had grown accustomed to her mother's library and assumed every household contained a few such volumes. "Do you suppose there's anything in that book that might tell me how to get rid of demons?" Mary Ann asked hopefully.

"I expect you'd have to call in a professional for that," Delia said. "Can't imagine where you'd find one, though. Are you Catholic, by any chance? I believe the Catholic Church still performs exorcism."

"No," Mary Ann told her. "Besides, I don't know how I'd explain that to Ted. Just imagine if he came home and found a stranger chanting and sprinkling holy water around the house."

"He does know about your concern, doesn't he?" Delia peered at her questioningly.

"Yes, of course. But he doesn't believe in ghosts

and such. Actually, I never did either, until now.
I'm not sure I do yet. But I don't know how else to
explain what's happening." Mary Ann suddenly
seemed on the verge of bursting into tears.

This alarmed Janet so greatly that she instinc-
tively reached over to pat Mary Ann's shoulder.
"We haven't established that you have a ghost in
your house. Perhaps Ted would be more likely to
get involved as well if you approached him from a
different stance. In fact, I think it would be a good
idea to begin with physical possibilities. Have your
house examined for structural defects that might
cause odd noises. It happens often, I believe."

"Good idea," Delia agreed. "Try the simplest explanation first. Meanwhile, you're welcome to bor-
row this book." She handed *Demons in Our Day*
across the table to Mary Ann. "You'll find that it
says in there the goal of the demon is to cause a
targeted individual to lose control of his or her will.
It wants to create fear and gain power. Seems to
me, whatever you've got to deal with has done a
pretty good job of getting to you. Hang tough. Be
stubborn. It works for Roger."

"Thank you, Delia." For the first time all morning Mary Ann smiled as if she meant it. "I really
appreciate the help."

"No prob. But for heaven's sake, keep me up-
dated. I want to know everything that happens
from here on. Oh, but don't mention this to just everybody. Folks around here have been looking for a
new one ever since Constance Winter went off to
the home. You don't want to become the leading
candidate."

"A new *what*?" Janet asked.

"Town loony," Delia said. "We just don't feel right
without at least one roaming the streets."

* * *

Reb Gassler had arrived almost half an hour before Sarah Elizabeth and her entourage returned from Memphis. Janet had been attempting to entertain the man in the kitchen of the Leach home and had found him to be quite congenial, once his natural reserve was softened by her sincere interest in his hometown. He had cleared up a number of minor mysteries for her, such as why the town's memorial statue looked like no one (a highly unethical voting procedure), why Delia's friend Roger was currently being shunned by half the county (his participation in the statue debacle), and why Pamela Satterfield flatly refused to take the hotline on Saturday nights (country music and buck dancing at the VFW hall).

Having ascertained that Janet was not a domestic violence volunteer, he had refused to give forth information about Melinda Forrest and her family until Sarah Elizabeth arrived. His grim face, however, did not hold promise of glad tidings.

Once the Leach family did arrive, it took some time to attend to important details such as Ariel's diaper and Sarah Elizabeth's headache. "I always have a killer headache when I get back from Memphis," she'd explained, gulping down two extra-strength aspirin. "Just let me rest a minute before you hit me with anything."

Reb complied by chatting quietly with her while Janet attended to Ariel's immediate needs. Eliza, feeling no need to treat law-enforcement officers with civility, pawed through the mail that Janet had stacked on the hall table, collected those pieces addressed to her, and retreated haughtily to her room.

Janet realized that her place in the house did not entitle her to join Sarah Elizabeth and Reb, but having been forced into a casual relationship with the family, she felt certain advantages ought to be available to her. Such as listening in on this particular conversation. With Ariel cleaned and dressed in warm pajamas, Janet carried the baby into the kitchen for her bedtime bottle. She arrived in time to catch Reb's opening statement.

"The medical examiner was able to narrow it down some," Reb was explaining. "Melinda went into the emergency room at six-twelve, according to the Medical Center's records. Her teenage daughter drove her there. I figure it takes twenty minutes to drive there from the Forrests' house. Melinda had been slapped around a good bit, of course, and she had a broken wrist. Nothing as bad as what's been done to her in the past."

Sarah Elizabeth nodded, knowing full well what injuries Melinda had sustained previously.

"Tad Hopkins found Forrest at right around six-thirty. James Forrest could have been shot anywhere from twenty to forty minutes earlier. You see the problem here?"

Again, Sarah Elizabeth nodded. "Melinda could have shot him before she left to go to the Medical Center. Fingerprints?"

"Big problem," Reb said. "Gun's missing. Whoever shot the man was thinking clearly enough to cover her tracks."

"Or *his* tracks," Sarah Elizabeth interjected.

"Yeah, okay. Forrest kept a .357 in the house and it's missing. Melinda would have known where he kept it."

"If he was attacking her, she had every reason to fear for her life. I can give you all sorts of expert testimony on that point. Self-defense is completely valid in this case."

"Excuse me," Janet interrupted, while shifting Ariel to her shoulder for burping. "Should you be discussing all this with Reb? He's rather on the other side, isn't he?"

Sarah Elizabeth glanced up, as if surprised to

find Janet sitting there. "Technically, yes. But our conversation is very definitely off the record." She gave Reb a look of warning. "Right?"

"Damn straight. I'd be in real big trouble if you ever told anybody I'd said I'da shot the SOB myself if I thought I could get away with it." Reb grinned at Sarah Elizabeth to assure her that her comments were safe with him.

"So . . . what are you going to do?"

Reb sighed regretfully. "I'm going to arrest the most likely suspect in the case. Can your group provide a lawyer for Mrs. Forrest?"

"With our funding? She'll have to take the public defender and hope for the best." Sarah Elizabeth, clearly disgusted with the situation and the system, kicked back her chair and rose to pour herself more coffee. After taking a moment to regain her composure, she returned to the table and sat uneasily on the edge of her chair. Turning to Janet, she said, "The girls will be staying here until Melinda is released. I'll increase your salary accordingly, Janet, since you'll obviously be stuck taking care of them. Maybe we can arrange bail for Melinda. Somehow." She did not seem optimistic about that possibility.

Reb rose slowly from his chair and, looking tenderly at Sarah Elizabeth, said, "I'm sorry."

"I know," she said quietly. "Call me if anything new comes up."

Pausing only to cast a lingering backward glance at Sarah Elizabeth, Reb strode out of the room. Janet heard the front door close as he left.

Having relieved herself of any possible digestive upset, Ariel was half-asleep on Janet's shoulder. The room, like the rest of the house, was uncomfortably silent. There seemed nothing to say that would not be either redundant or ridiculous, so

Janet rocked softly while Sarah Elizabeth stared broodingly into her half-empty coffee mug.

Then, from the distance of the hall, came the tap-tapping of Eliza's feet on the stairs. A few more steps and she stood, wild-eyed and red-faced in the doorway, like a glowering prophetess of doom. Waving a sheet of paper in front of her with one hand, she pointed a bony finger at Janet with the other.

"This . . ." she said, obviously struggling for an appropriate word, *"woman!"*

"What now, Mother Eliza?" Sarah Elizabeth demanded. Her tone bordered on snappish.

"This woman is a fraud!" Eliza announced.

"I've had enough!" Placing her hands firmly on the table, Sarah Elizabeth shoved herself into standing position and turned to face her mother-in-law. "You are absolutely driving me mad. Janet was hired at your insistence. She is doing an excellent job of caring for Ariel, and how she puts up with you and me and the rest of this madhouse, I do not know. But let me tell you one thing—if you so much as look hard at her in the future, I'm going to have *you* locked up with your crazy son. Do you understand me?"

Apparently Eliza did not understand or did not care, for she continued to glare at Janet. "Explain this," she demanded, holding out the paper for Janet to read. "Nanny Cares Training Center informs me that they have never—mind you, *never*—had a trainee named Janet Ayres. Just who are you, young woman?"

"Mother Eliza, how dare you accuse Janet—"

"Wait, Sarah Elizabeth." Janet handed the paper back to Eliza. "She's right, actually. I *am* a fraud."

Had the proverbial pin dropped at that moment, it would have sounded like a wrecking ball in the Leach kitchen. Even little Ariel seemed to catch her breath in surprise.

Normally a calm and collected woman, Janet felt a wave of pure cowardice wash over her. For that reason she turned her back to the elder Mrs. Leach and made her confession to Sarah Elizabeth, who seemed too stunned to pose a threat. "My mother attended the Woodstock music festival," she said, hoping that no other explanation would be called for. The lack of comprehension in Sarah Elizabeth's eyes was disappointing and Janet realized that she would have to reveal the whole sordid story.

Gathering courage even as her self-respect dwindled, she went on. "It was an event punctuated by many lapses of judgment and self-control. Shortly afterward, my mother discovered that she was pregnant. For reasons known only to her, she chose to remain single. She also chose to name me"— Janet paused, squeezing her eyes shut as if she could not bear to see the reaction to her revelation—"Flowering Peach Child-of-Earth."

"You're kidding," Sarah Elizabeth said, as if she truly believed a person might joke about a name like that.

"Unfortunately, no. That, Mrs. Leach, is my name. If you contact Nanny Cares again and ask for my records under that name, you will find that I graduated with honors. What's more, I believe my instructors will give me excellent recommendations."

"You're kidding," Sarah Elizabeth repeated, then giggled. "Flowering Peach? Was your mother from Jesus Creek, by any chance?"

Janet could not help an involuntary shudder. "Naturally I could not face playmates with such a name. Children are brutal and I'm sure you can imagine what I would have suffered through. Since my mother is, and always has been, a free spirit— meaning she flits from town to town, philosophy to philosophy—I was actually raised by my maternal

grandparents, Bill and Freida Ayres. My grandmother was inordinately fond of the Lennon Sis-
ters, particularly the youngest girl. It was she who
wisely insisted on renaming me, at least infor-
mally."

"Your mother actually calls you Flowering
Peach?" Sarah Elizabeth wanted to know.

"These days she calls me F.P. Which is a great
improvement over Peachie."

"What nonsense!" Eliza said, with a superior
sniff. "I do not believe a word of it. Sarah Elizabeth, call the police this instant and inform them of
this person's criminal intentions."

"What criminal intentions, Mother Eliza?"

"Obviously she is trying to kidnap little Lindsay.
Why else would she concoct this fantastic story to
insinuate herself into our good graces? Not, mind
you, that I was fooled for a minute. Breeding tells,
young woman." Eliza shook a bony finger at Janet.
"The lower classes are incapable of passing themselves off as quality people. It's in the blood."

"Mrs. Leach, I assure you, I would never attempt
to harm Ariel. And I most certainly am not a criminal!" Janet protested.

"Mother Eliza, go to bed," Sarah Elizabeth said
firmly. "I'll personally stand guard over Janet tonight to be sure she doesn't abscond with the family silver *or* my daughter."

"May I remind you," Eliza said, "that little
Lindsay is the last of the Leach line? A great many
people have reasons to want this family destroyed."

"You ain't kidding," Sarah Elizabeth muttered.
Aloud she said, "Go to bed. I'll take care of it."

With a last killing look at Janet, Eliza whipped
out of the room and stomped her way up the stairs.

"Don't worry," Sarah Elizabeth said, "she'll be
over it by morning. The kidnapping part, anyway.

By tomorrow she'll have figured out that you're guilty of a really big crime."

"Excuse me?" Janet asked with alarm.

"Denying your birthright."

POSSESSION

CHAPTER

7

October 12

Dear Papaw,

I appreciate the care you have taken to protect me, but it will no longer be necessary to forward my mail in new envelopes. The Leach family (and no doubt the entire town) is aware of the awful truth and have been for almost two weeks now. With a few exceptions, I have encountered no ridicule or scorn. Only the elder Mrs. Leach seems disturbed, but she never liked me anyway.

You'll recall that our neighbor was experiencing what she believed to be supernormal phenomena. Another resident has given her a book on the subject and I hope, although I have not read it myself, that it will encourage her to seek out rational explanations for the events she has witnessed. I have seen little of her these past days, but not for want of effort. Twice we have planned day trips, and both times she has canceled. Claiming illness or an unexpected engage-

ment on Ted's behalf, she excuses herself from
these and future plans. Actually she was eager, I
felt, until her husband pointed out that she was
not feeling well enough to go out or until he
asked her to make a special dinner for business
acquaintances. I suppose he might disapprove of
her friendship with me, although I cannot imagine on what grounds.

The children who were staying with us when I
first arrived are here again, this time for even
more unfortunate reasons. The mother, Melinda,
is charged with murdering her abusive husband.
I gather that law-enforcement officials are fully
aware of the violent history, yet Melinda is forced
to linger in jail until bail is provided (this seems
unlikely to happen soon) or until she is found innocent of the charge. There is little doubt that
she did, indeed, kill her husband, but I believe a
plea of self-defense will find favor with any jury.
The children are, need I tell you, having a difficult time adjusting. While Katrina, the younger
daughter, has made herself quite at home, only
occasionally asking about her mother, the teenage daughter, Leesha, is all but maddened by
grief. One man, it seems, has victimized not only
the wife he assaulted, but also the children and
friends of the family.

Henry Mooten has taken to visiting from time
to time and during our brief conversations I have
learned a good deal about him. None of it reassuring, incidentally, but knowledge is power, or
so they say. I only hope that I will not be called
to testify against him someday when his sanity
hearing is held. Generally he walks over from his
second residence, the diner, and always carries a
backpack, which he refers to as his survival kit.
This is a habit he acquired some months ago
while waiting for an earthquake to strike. As I've

mentioned, however, he no longer rants about acts of God or extraterrestrial invasions, but rather focuses his attention these days on anything that might be construed as unusual. How he can recognize such is beyond me.

He was kind enough to offer to drive me home last week when my daily stroll was interrupted by a brief but pounding rainstorm. I have learned that when he drives, Mr. Mooten travels in a 1960 Valiant with vacuum windshield wipers that work once. Therefore, if he wants to remove rain from his front window, he is forced to sit forward in the driver's seat (Mr. Mooten is not a tall man) and manually switch the wipers on then off then on then off, etc. The door on the driver's side does not close properly, so he has cleverly tied that together with a wire hanger and makes his entrances and exits through the passenger's door. I overheard him mention to Sarah Elizabeth that the leak in the window is worse, causing a good inch of water to sit pooled in the floor of his car. This, he says, freezes over in the winter and one must be especially careful not to rest one's feet there, as the car's heater does not work at all and pneumonia is a possibility. The finishing touch is his bumper sticker, which reads: MY TWO BEST FRIENDS ARE JACK AND CHARLIE DANIELS.

Other members of this quaint community have begun to welcome me, for which I am sometimes grateful. Pamela Satterfield, Sarah Elizabeth's employee at the library and one of the most dependable SAN volunteers, invited me to join her and the deputy police chief, German Hunt, for an evening of dancing. Naturally I was reluctant, as I have no suitable clothing for such a gala event. My worries, of course, were pointless. It seems dancing in Jesus Creek is limited to the weekly hoedown at the VFW hall. Having known Pamela

only in a more formal setting, I was somewhat
amused to see her doing what is known as the
Texas Two-Step in the middle of a room full of
two-steppers, all of them singing along with various country-western tunes. (Have you had occasion to listen to the lyrics of these songs?) By
evening's end I, too, had learned to two-step in
such a way as to make any Texan proud, and several of the unattached men in attendance have
expressed an interest in escorting me to the next
dance. I mention this only so that you will understand I am not "shriveling up like a prune." I
certainly have no intention of accepting any such
invitation.

Meanwhile I continue my struggle with the un-
orthodox Leach household. Little Ariel is thriving
under my care and rolls merrily from front to
back to front again during our scheduled play-
time. Her mother is diligent in displaying affection for the child, although I sometimes feel that
a lengthy vacation from motherhood would do
Sarah Elizabeth a world of good.

Mother's recent lack of correspondence sug-
gests to me that she is on the move again. Generally it takes a few weeks for her to find her
new calling and settle into enthusiastic expression of it. No doubt we will be hearing from her
soon.

All my love,
Janet

It fell to Janet to escort Katrina and Leesha to
their home in order to collect clothing and personal
items for use during their stay with Sarah Elizabeth. Following Leesha's directions, Janet steered
the gigantic Leach car into a rutted driveway on

the outskirts of Angela County and up to the front
door of an unassuming frame house.

This was not the domicile Janet would have
tagged for domestic violence. While the yard was
bare of everything but grass and two untrimmed
shrubs, it was generally well tended and contained
not a single rusted-out automobile. No mangy mon-
grels greeted them with snarls, nor was the path
littered with empty beer cans. To the casual eye,
this appeared to be a perfectly normal house.

Entering through the front door, Janet and Ariel
waited in the living room while Leesha took her
younger sister into the back of the house to collect
their belongings. An open doorway leading to the
kitchen caught her attention. This, she reasoned,
must have been where the body of James Forrest
had been found. She could not help but wonder
whether Forrest had attempted to reach a telephone or had died instantly from his wounds. An
inner voice unrelated to her normally sensitive nature whispered a hope that he had, indeed, lived
long enough to suffer and to regret his past behavior.

Leesha's efficiency, probably heightened by her
obvious reluctance to spend time in the house, got
them in and out in short order. Tossing a single
suitcase into the trunk, Janet reminded the girls to
fasten their seat belts. Fixing Ariel securely in the
child-safety seat, she then turned to Leesha. "Shall
we pick up your car in the hospital parking lot? Or
has it been removed already?"

"As far as I know, it's still there," Leesha said. "I
guess we'd better get it before somebody tears it
up."

"Don't forget the keys," Katrina reminded her.

"Oh, that's right. The keys are still in Mom's
purse, back at Sarah Elizabeth's. Well, never mind.

I'll just walk over to the Medical Center later and get it. We can go on home now."

"An excellent suggestion. If there are no objections," Janet said, starting the car and backing out the driveway, "we will carve jack-o'-lanterns this afternoon. I have noticed that a great many of them have already begun to appear about town."

The abundance of Halloween decorations surprised her not at all. Jesus Creek was a town that revered ghosts and their trappings. Only Mary Ann Thorn seemed disturbed by them. But then, she was an outsider and did not appreciate the honor of having ancestral specters roaming about her home.

Janet nearly drove into a ditch when she realized that *outsider* had come to her as a derisive term.

The preschool child, Janet had quickly learned, is something of a leech, sucking energy and time from those adults foolish enough to allow themselves to become hosts for the parasite. Katrina, no doubt as a result of the lack of appropriate parental figures in her life, had attached herself to Janet with a flattering, if exhausting, devotion. Recognizing the child's need for love and attention, Janet would not have been surprised to find that Katrina resented Ariel, but instead she merely ignored the baby.

Leesha, on the other hand, had appointed herself mother-protector and spent most of her time with Ariel in arms. Sarah Elizabeth practically had to beg for time with her own daughter.

"I'll hold Ariel. You go ahead," Leesha had insisted at lunch, and again afterward when the entire household sans Eliza had gathered on the front porch to decorate for the upcoming holiday.

"But wouldn't you like to carve a pumpkin?" Sarah Elizabeth said.

"No, really. I don't mind." And Leesha had hugged Ariel a little tighter. "Why don't you and

Janet help Katrina with hers? She'll want to carve it herself and you'll have to keep a close eye on her. She's too little for a knife, but she's stubborn as a mule."

This Janet had already learned and knew that Katrina would insist on creating her own ghoulish jack-o'-lantern. "Very well," the nanny conceded. "Leesha, dress Ariel warmly and bring her outside. Sarah Elizabeth and I will supervise Katrina." Hustling everyone outside, Janet quickly spread newspaper and pencils on the porch, then began explaining to Katrina the importance of proper design planning.

"I don't want to interfere," Sarah Elizabeth said from her place on the porch swing, "but I don't think she's going to listen to you."

In fact, Katrina was already digging into the skin of the pumpkin, totally ignoring Janet's instruction.

"No, wait, Katrina," Janet pleaded. "First remove the top and pull out the seeds and pulp. Here, I'll help." Deftly removing the pumpkin from Katrina's pudgy hands, Janet sliced off the top and used her knife to loosen the meat. "Now, just reach in there and pull out all that yucky stuff."

"Having Katrina here has done wonders for you, Janet," Sarah Elizabeth said with a grin. "I don't believe I've ever heard you use the word *yucky* before."

"Unfortunately Katrina's vocabulary has been shaped by her mother and older sister. In order to communicate, I am forced to speak a language she understands. With time, I hope to influence her communication skills significantly."

"Oh," Sarah Elizabeth said, still amused. "Good luck."

By the time Leesha joined them, Katrina had advanced to the actual carving of eyes and a nose, all slightly lopsided, but nonetheless effective. From

time to time she would stare malevolently at the
pumpkin and shout, "Boo!"

"Be careful with that knife," Leesha said instinc-
tively, stepping around the pumpkin innards that
Katrina had spread about the porch. Joining Sarah
Elizabeth on the swing, she held up Ariel for her
mother's inspection. "Isn't she just darling this
morning? I swear I heard her say *mama* just now."

"She's bright, but she's no genius, Leesha,"
Sarah Elizabeth insisted. "I don't think she'll be
talking until she's at least five months old." Her attempt to retrieve her daughter failed, and she settled for gazing adoringly at the baby in Leesha's
lap.

"We'll be able to visit your mother this afternoon." Sarah Elizabeth spoke softly, as if hoping a
neutral tone would avoid reminders of the need for
observing visiting hours at the jail.

"As soon as Katrina's finished making her mess,
I'll get her cleaned up," Leesha said. Then, offhand-
edly, she added, "Mother is innocent. She keeps
telling them that. I don't know why they won't let
her go."

"Of course she is," Sarah Elizabeth said with sincerity. "It's red tape and legal procedure. Unfortunately the timing of your father's death came so
soon after you'd all left the house . . . but never
mind. Her lawyer will take care of the explanations. It's important for you and Katrina to keep
your mother's spirits up."

"What would it take," Leesha asked, "to get
Mom freed?"

"Well," Sarah Elizabeth said, "a witness who
saw someone go into the house after you drove your
mother to the hospital. That would be pretty
darned effective."

"But not Mr. Hopkins?"

Tad Hopkins, an old drinking buddy of James

Forrest's, had been the one to find the body. He'd sauntered through the front door of the Forrest house around six-thirty, beer in hand, and called out to the dead man. It had taken him little time to figure out that he wasn't going to get a reply. James Forrest's body had been sprawled across the living-room floor, the effect of a single gun blast to the chest evident to Hopkins even in his advanced stage of inebriation.

"He can't help, Leesha," Sarah Elizabeth said as if apologizing for this fact. "Mr. Hopkins got there far too late to see who did it."

"But what if—" Leesha broke off as Katrina made a vicious stab at her pumpkin's mouth. "Katrina, watch out!"

"Not to worry," Janet replied. "I replaced her carving knife with a butter knife as soon as the jack-o'-lantern was complete. She's just playing now."

Leesha breathed a sigh of obvious relief, while Sarah Elizabeth shook her head. Janet was getting the hang of child care quickly.

Sarah Elizabeth had promised to treat the Forrest girls to lunch at Eloise's Diner after the visit to Melinda. She had understandably chosen to leave Ariel in Janet's care, rather than drag the baby along to the jail.

It had taken most of the day, but Janet had at last contrived an excuse to visit Mary Ann. While she had mentioned her misgivings to no one, not even to her grandfather, Janet was not at all certain that Mary Ann was doing well.

In the past two weeks Janet had not once seen Mary Ann outside her house. Ted had driven off each morning, returned each evening, and made several irregular trips throughout the weekends. But Mary Ann and the baby were not to be seen.

Fearing that her interest might be interpreted as nosiness, Janet had refrained from intercepting Ted when she'd seen him outside. Her own life had suddenly grown uncontrollably busy and there simply had been no time for a visit to the neighbor. Janet only hoped that Mary Ann was busy with domestic chores and not ill.

She had watched the Thorn house carefully but discreetly all day and finally decided that action must be taken. Wrapping a heavy blanket around Ariel, Janet headed across the yard. Mary Ann's vandalized car still sat in the driveway, like the remnant of an ancient civilization. Why it seemed ominous, Janet could not say.

There was no sound of child or television or of life coming from the house as Janet knocked timidly at the back door. She did not hear Mary Ann's footsteps approach and so was doubly shocked when the door was suddenly wrenched open and her neighbor stood before her.

Mary Ann's eyes were underlined by heavy dark circles. Her hair, while neatly groomed, was dull and lifeless, as was Mary Ann overall. The woman showed no emotion at finding Janet on her doorstep, merely stepped back and motioned her inside.

"Mary Ann, you look terrible!" Janet cried. "Have you been ill?"

"No," Mary Ann said tonelessly. "I'm fine."

"That's obviously untrue," Janet said without leniency. "You look as if you haven't slept in weeks. You're pale, you're trembling, and you're clearly tense." She pulled out a kitchen chair and seated herself firmly, making it obvious to anyone watching that she intended to stay until satisfied. "Now, tell me what's wrong."

Mary Ann slumped against the counter. "It's the same thing, Janet," she said with a resigned sigh.

"It goes on and on. Look over there." She pointed to the back door.

Janet, following Mary Ann's direction, glanced over her shoulder. Just above the doorknob she could see scratches, as if someone had tried to claw an opening in the door.

"I found it this morning," Mary Ann explained weakly. "I wake up at night and there's a weight on my chest, like someone sitting on me. Someone evil and—oh, I don't know." She shook her head as if disgusted with her own story. "I must be crazy. No one else sees anything, no one hears anything. There's nothing there. I look all over the house and it's empty."

"Has Delia's book been at all useful?" Janet asked.

"The book!" Mary Ann turned suddenly frantic and whirled around to the counter. She pulled out a drawer and pawed through it until at last she pulled out *Demons in Our Day*. "Ted almost spotted it this morning. Give this back to Delia for me, will you? I just don't know when I'll have time to go over there myself."

"Of course," Janet said, taking the book and tucking it into her lap beneath Ariel. "Was it of any help to you?"

"No," Mary Ann said quickly. "I'm sorry. I'll make some coffee. I'm glad you came over. I've been meaning to call, but I'm so busy all the time. This house won't stay clean for anything, and Eddie's had a little cold."

Janet watched suspiciously as Mary Ann bustled about the kitchen, filling the coffee maker and chattering inconsequential pleasantries. It was obvious from her neighbor's sudden change of mood that she did not wish to discuss the book or the disturbing situation at hand. Janet would not push her, then. She had come prepared with a story and hoped that turning the conversation might help Mary Ann to relax. Later, when they'd had coffee and grown comfortable, she would approach the possibility of counseling.

"Sarah Elizabeth has been so busy lately," Janet began. "You know, of course, that we have extra children in the house now."

"Oh, yes," Mary Ann said, taking cups from the cabinet. "The Forrest girls. I heard about that. Isn't it just awful? But I guess that's what happens when these women don't get out."

"What do you mean?" Janet asked.

"Well, if that Mrs. Forrest had left the first time he hit her, it never would have come to this, would it? Now she's killed the man and her daughters don't have a family anymore. That's so sad for the little girls. Families need to be together."

"It's sad, of course. But Mrs. Forrest insists, first of all, that she did not kill her husband. And frankly, if she *did*, I can understand why. Sarah Elizabeth has told me absolute horror stories about the way the woman's been treated."

Mary Ann, hanging over the coffeepot as if willing it to perk faster, shook her head. "Well, like I said, if she'd left the first time he hit her, it wouldn't have happened. I can tell you one thing—if Ted ever laid a hand on me, I'd whop him upside the head with an iron skillet."

Janet, having been indoctrinated by Sarah Elizabeth and the other SAN volunteers, found herself unable to dismiss the problem that easily. "Mr. Forrest was quite a large man, I believe. Had his wife attempted to fight back, she might well have received even worse injuries."

"Well, he had to sleep sometime, didn't he?" Mary Ann asked.

"There are other factors, Mary Ann. Melinda had been—well, brainwashed, if you will. Experiments have been done, in which a dog receives an electric shock whenever it attempts to leave its cage. After a while the dog will not try to leave the cage at all, because of training and fear. Melinda is much like that. She had come to think of her home as a prison and her husband as a guard who could inflict pain and injury whenever he chose. Like the test animal, she felt that cowering in a corner was her only safe choice."

"Come on, Janet. She got out of the house to go grocery shopping, didn't she? Why didn't she just stay gone?"

"Also," Janet went on, "I am told that victims of domestic violence are often at greater risk after they leave the abuser. Perhaps Mrs. Forrest felt that her chances of survival were better if she stayed with him."

"That's what these safe houses are for," Mary Ann pointed out. "She didn't have to leave Sarah Elizabeth's and go back to him."

Janet could not argue with that. The psychological aspects of the case had eluded her, too. She had to admit that parroting what she'd learned from Sarah Elizabeth and other SAN volunteers did not make it acceptable truth. Believing that self-preservation was of prime importance, Janet had tried and failed to understand why Melinda Forrest hadn't made her escape when it was possible.

"I must agree with you. Of course, Sarah Elizabeth or one of the other volunteers might be able to explain Mrs. Forrest's actions. Unfortunately a great many of the volunteers have, for one reason or another, left the program. Sarah Elizabeth was saying just the other day that the hotline may have to be handed over to an answering service."

"Really?" Mary Ann said without interest as she poured their coffee. "I wonder why they didn't do that in the first place?"

"According to Sarah Elizabeth, most of the callers who use the hotline are seeking counseling or information or merely a friendly voice. The answering service will not be able to provide this. I believe that somehow SAN will have to round up a new crop of volunteers. Which brings me to the reason for my visit. Might you be interested?"

"Me?" Mary Ann seemed positively shocked. "Good heavens, I wouldn't know what to say to those women! I'd just tell them to kill the so-and-so and be done with it."

"Well, of course, you'd need training. I think you'd be quite good at this. And since you don't work outside the home, it would be relatively easy for you to schedule in a day for hotline service."

Mary Ann sat down across from Janet, apparently considering the idea. "Maybe I will," she said at last. "I'll think it over."

Janet was pleased with herself. She had not really expected Mary Ann to agree and had only used the dearth of volunteers as a convenient excuse to visit her. Happily, she now seemed to have done a great favor for Sarah Elizabeth and SAN.

"You seem to be feeling better already," Janet pointed out. And it was true. Mary Ann's nervousness had diminished somewhat and her eyes were focusing more clearly than they had upon Janet's arrival. "Perhaps you've been cooped up here at home too long. I suggest that we take an afternoon for ourselves and go out for dinner. I'd prefer to avoid Eloise's, if that's possible, but I believe they serve pizza at the Drink Tank."

"Oh, I'd like that," Mary Ann said, obviously setting up a refusal. "But we just can't afford it. Ted is having fits about the budget. He's even had to cut back on my grocery money. I don't know how on earth I'm going to make the grocery budget stretch."

"Well, then. Why don't we at least take a walk? Fresh air would do you good. I'm sure Eddie and Ariel would enjoy it, too."

Mary Ann shook her head. "I think not, Janet. I'm just too tired, and Eddie's been sniffling all day. I finally got him to take a nap a few minutes ago and I'd hate to wake him. Besides, the chilly weather would only make his cold worse."

Janet might have pointed out that colds are caused by germs, not by fresh air, but it was clear that Mary Ann would then be forced to invent another excuse for staying home. While a change of scenery might be the best thing for her, Janet could not think of a single attraction sufficient to lure her out of the house. "Maybe tomorrow, then," she said, finishing her coffee.

Before Mary Ann could make a polite reply, the wall phone behind her jangled. Mary Ann jumped to answer it, as if she'd been expecting an emergency call all along. Grabbing the receiver before the first ring had died away, she breathed, "Hello." After a pause, she replaced the receiver and slumped back against the counter.

"Mary Ann? Is something wrong?" Janet asked, instantly alarmed.

Looking out through the kitchen window with an expression between anger and terror, Mary Ann replied, "There was no one there."

"Wrong numbers can be so irritating, can't they?" Janet agreed.

"It's not a wrong number!" Mary Ann turned on her, practically crying. "It happens all the time. Someone is doing this to me on purpose."

There seemed little chance of convincing her that telephone pranksters were not necessarily intent upon driving her nuts, so Janet did not try. Instead, she shifted Ariel to a more comfortable position and waited uneasily while Mary Ann refilled her cup.

"It happens so often lately," Mary Ann said. Glancing at the mutilated door, she picked up her coffee and set the pot on the Formica counter.

"Mary Ann!" Janet said, pointing to the pot. "You'll burn that."

"What? Oh." Mary Ann removed the pot to its proper location, as if it mattered not a whit to her. "Silly me."

What seemed to Mary Ann a minor incident worried Janet greatly. Absentminded behavior was one thing when it involved misplacing a glove. It was quite another when that behavior might lead to a dangerous or even fatal accident.

Demons in Our Day was not the sort of book Janet normally read. For that matter, Mary Ann was not the sort of friend Janet normally made, either. But if Mary Ann would not read the book and at last *try* to understand her problem, Janet felt it her duty to look into the matter.

She had left the book in her room until the evening's chores were complete. Ariel had been fed, bathed, and tucked snugly into her crib. Eliza, still keeping to her room, had demanded that Sarah Elizabeth bring her dinner on a tray. It seemed she had decided that Janet was not only a kidnapper, but a poisoner as well, and had refused to eat a bite until Sarah Elizabeth tasted everything on the tray.

Leesha and Katrina confined themselves to the rec room, watching television and eating their dinners on trays. Sarah Elizabeth had offered to join them, but their acceptance had been so lukewarm, she'd remained in the kitchen, ultimately feeding most of her dinner to the puppy.

It was late before Janet could settle into her own room and she wondered if it would be wise to stay awake reading. But while her body was exhausted, her mind would not stop circling the riddle of Mary Anne's strange and ominous behavior. At last she chose reading over endless speculation.

The author began with a long and boring account of demon possession. Janet had not known that such a silly subject could be made to sound so uninteresting and she finally opted to skip the introduction and a chapter on spiritual definitions of demons. Turning to the middle of the book, she found more useful information.

As she had recalled from her mother's babbling on the subject, a house most often was possessed by an evil spirit when someone in that house invited the spirit in, as through communication with the dead via Ouija board or some other vehicle. And of course there was the always popular theory that houses might be possessed by the restless ghost of a former inhabitant.

Stifling for the moment her scorn of the very possibility of possession, Janet made a guess at the age of the Thorn house. Surely not more than fifteen or twenty years old, it had most recently been inhabited by a friendly farm couple of whom Delia Cannon approved. Had a tragedy occurred in the house before that, Delia would surely have known and mentioned it. Temporarily ruling out the unhappy ghost as vandal and prankster, Janet moved on.

Under what circumstances might Mary Ann or Ted have invited the trouble into their home? Janet could think of none, but recognized her lack of expertise in the area. Might someone else have done it? Henry Mooten and his friend had mentioned devil worshipers gathering in a field—Henry, of course, had chalked the evidence up to UFO landing gear, but never mind that bit of nonsense. Not that devil worship wasn't nonsense, too, but if she carried that thought to its logical conclusion, a haunted house was no less ridiculous.

Deciding that the origin of the trouble might better be left to another time, Janet continued reading. The book provided a list of symptoms that marked the early stages of infestation. These were along the lines of the events Mary Ann had experienced: lights turning on and off by themselves, small items disappearing only to reappear again without explanation, odors without cause, disembodied voices.

It was not reassuring to discover, in the next chapter, that Mary Ann had reached Stage Two of the process. During the oppression stage, the invading force would seek to create fear in the human inhabitants, dividing them against each other and breaking their wills. In essence, it sought to cause loss of control and dehumanization of the victim.

Mary Ann's tension, her reluctance to take on the simple task of a shopping trip or answering the hotline, her lack of interest in her appearance—all these might well signal her declining self-esteem. Dissociative behavior, such as setting a coffeepot on a Formica countertop, seemed an extreme example of the symptoms described.

Janet could not help glancing out her window, as if she wanted to verify that the house next door still stood dark and silent. Nothing seemed out of the ordinary, no howls or inhuman screams greeted her. To all appearances, the Thorn house would look normal and comfortable to a casual observer.

Reluctantly turning a page, Janet began the chapter on Stage Three, which was described as demonic possession of the victim. This might appear, the author told her, to be extreme anxiety (which certainly was observable in Mary Ann) or sudden panic attacks. The victim might seem out of contact with the real world, perhaps being startled by a touch or a loud voice. The incidents that in earlier stages had been frustrating but benign would now become more threatening, sometimes leading to physical injury.

Certainly Mary Ann had injuries to show. Her throat was proof that Stage Three had begun. Janet's hand went involuntarily to her own throat as she read the rest of the chapter.

CHAPTER

8

IT WAS A MOMENT OF RARE PLEASURE—
sitting quietly in the kitchen, with only the puppy
for company and a cup of hot cocoa within easy
reach. A wall clock ticked off seconds in a soothing
rhythm, accompanied by the intermittent drip of
the faucet. Janet had not realized until that moment how much she missed privacy and the comfort of a kitchen with wandering Jew hanging in
the window.

Her grandfather's early bedtime had afforded her
many such moments at home, but one could not
stay wrapped in the cocoon of one's family forever.
There had been no useful excuse to keep her
there—her grandfather's health was excellent, so
he needed no caretaker to watch over him. In another family, the only grandchild might have opted
to reside near the family for unity's sake, but hers
most certainly was not a traditional family. Besides, her mother's many departures throughout
the years had not seemed to take an emotional toll
on her grandfather. In fact, he'd always seemed a
bit relieved when she left. That was Mother, of

course, and almost anyone would find her absence refreshing. Perhaps her grandfather *did* miss Janet. If so, he'd given no indication that he was anything less than proud and supportive of her decision to find her way in the world.

Wrapped in her house robe, feet propped on a chair, with the timid puppy peeking through the door at her, she felt an urge to see Papaw, to chat quietly with him about nothing in particular, to go home again. It took several minutes of positive reinforcement to convince herself that she *was* home. "Come on, pooch," she whispered at last. Removing herself from the chair, Janet sat tailor-fashion on the floor and held out her hand. "Come on. You can sit in my lap and I'll scratch your chin."

The dog seemed undecided, edging its nose toward her, then backing away. Janet would have thought the shadows of the laundry room intimidating, but the puppy seemed to take comfort in them tonight. Perhaps the mutt had successfully made those shadows home. A lesson could be learned, Janet decided. Her mother was fond of quoting a wall plaque she'd once seen: BLOOM WHERE YOU'RE PLANTED. But did she really want to settle for safety and comfort in a dark, damp world? Which Jesus Creek most certainly was. She would have to take stock of her own situation and determine whether remaining in Jesus Creek would be an enlightening, educational, eventually positive experience, or simply a resting place in which she'd chosen to hide. It was too soon to tell whether her unrest was caused by lack of adjustment or genuine discomfort, and Janet knew from experience that she must not act too quickly. She was a creature of habit, perhaps a bit stuffy. This did not seem to her an altogether unfortunate trait.

The puppy had made its decision. A sudden movement of Janet's arm sent the animal scurrying behind the dryer. "Be sensible," Janet told it sternly. "You can't hide forever. I'm not going to hurt you, you silly creature. Now come out here and make friends."

She rose slowly and crept quietly through the door, into the laundry room with its row of muslined windows letting in just enough moonlight to make the appliances discernible. She could reach behind the dryer far enough to grasp a puppy leg or tail and drag the miserable mutt out again. There was a time, she thought, to let the puppy whimper and a time to force it out into the world. If left to itself, the animal would never conquer its fear of humans.

As she bent over from the waist, her arm stretched full length and almost within reach of the animal, something else caught her attention. It was only a flash and Janet was not at all certain she'd actually seen it. Perhaps her peripheral vision had caught a ghost light from the fluorescent above the kitchen sink reflected off the laundry-room windows. Still, she had the distinct impression that what she'd seen had come from beyond the windows, from outside.

Pulling the puppy out of its hiding place and gathering it in her arms, she straightened just enough to be able to peer outside. Drawing back the muslin curtain that shielded the window, she surveyed the darkened yard. The boundaries of Leach property were defined by boxwood and birch trees planted at carefully calculated intervals. At first there was nothing but the blackness of the autumn night. And then, when her eyes had adjusted, she was able to make out the shapes of trees and shrubbery, and the nearly dilapidated garden shed in the center of the yard.

Beside that, still as any of the other objects, Janet recognized the shape of a human being. It stood perfectly still, apparently unaware of Janet's presence. Without thought or hesitation, she withdrew into the kitchen, still clutching the nervous puppy.

Time seemed to drag as she dialed 911 and waited through four rings before a sleepy voice answered.

"There is a prowler in my yard," she said quietly. "The address is 240 Primrose Lane."

"That the Leach house?" the dispatcher asked.

"Yes, it is. Please send an officer immediately."

"Sure thang" was the reply. "Stay low and I'll have somebody there 'fore you can say Jack Spratt."

While Janet had never before had occasion to call the police emergency line, she nevertheless was surprised at how calmly the dispatcher had received her news. If he was familiar with Sarah Elizabeth's address, one would think he might have recognized the potential for disaster her news presented and reacted with a bit more energy. A stranger lurking in the darkness in any other yard might be nothing more than a misplaced insomniac. In the Leach yard, it was entirely possible that the stranger was a deranged and homicidal husband.

Sarah Elizabeth needed to be notified, she realized, and headed upstairs to wake her employer. A good night's sleep would have been of great benefit to them all, but clearly that would not come tonight. Knowing the power of adrenaline, Janet suspected that even after the problem here was resolved, no one would feel the slightest twinge of drowsiness. Still, if the police performed efficiently, they would sleep better tomorrow night, knowing that the person who'd been stalking them was at last in custody.

Sarah Elizabeth came awake quickly and, without bothering to dress, followed Janet downstairs. She did not ask why Janet was holding the puppy, obviously against its will and in spite of the claw marks it continued to inflict on her arms. "We'll try not to bother the others," Sarah Elizabeth whispered. "I'll bet anything this is Missy's husband."

"I would not be at all surprised," Janet agreed. "However, I suspect that he will not stand around the yard waiting to be captured once the police have made their presence known. While I do not suggest that we attempt to apprehend him ourselves, it might be advisable to keep an eye on him from the back windows. We may be able to get a good look at his face when he bolts, thus allowing us to identify him later."

"Good idea. Let's go." Sarah Elizabeth led the way cautiously through the kitchen and into the laundry room, stooping to keep most of her body below window level. "Don't stand too close to the window," she cautioned. "And be perfectly still. Even if he sees our heads, he may mistake us for furniture."

It was not until they had positioned themselves that the puppy, in a burst of nervousness, bolted from Janet's arms to scurry behind the washer. Janet was surprised—not at her own forgetfulness, but rather at the sense of emptiness she felt now that her arms were free.

For some minutes the women stood in absolute silence, each wondering if the menacing figure they watched would turn and spot them. If that happened, there was a good chance he would run. Disappointing as that would be—for both wanted this prowler captured—it was preferable to having him pull a weapon and fire in their direction. Sarah Elizabeth, at least, knew that this, too, was a possibility. They waited silently, neither daring to move or speak, lest the man outside notice.

Just as Janet was on the verge of admitting aloud that the motionless shadow she'd taken for a human being might be nothing more than a shrub, it moved. One arm raised slightly, a brief movement followed by a tiny flare of light, told them that their stalker was enjoying a cigarette. He did not appear to be concerned about exposure.

"Cocky, isn't he?" Sarah Elizabeth whispered.

Janet did not reply, even though she was in full agreement and found it disturbing that their prowler was so confident.

It was Sarah Elizabeth who first spotted the second figure. This one approached from the opposite side of the yard, carefully moving through the darkness and the row of privacy hedge toward the first man.

"There's two of them," Janet whispered. "In taking care to conceal ourselves from one, I hope we haven't been entirely obvious to the second."

"No, that one's Reb. Bless his heart, he came on foot. We're lucky German didn't show up. He uses his siren even if he's just going to get a kitten out of a tree."

Now that she had been told the identity of the second figure, it was easy for Janet to recognize his massive frame. He moved with a grace she would not have expected from so large a man, gliding smoothly across the lawn, one hand firmly in contact with his still-holstered gun. She watched as Reb eased against the shed, gauging his distance from the prowler by the cigarette's glowing tip. With agonizing care, Reb moved along the side of the structure, slowly around the front, and finally to the corner, just inches from where the prowler stood.

The man was taken completely by surprise. Janet assumed that was why he put up no resistance when Reb at last rounded the corner of the building and shouted "Hey!" loud enough to be heard across two counties.

Once Reb had cornered the perpetrator, Sarah Elizabeth darted out the door in a flash, with Janet close on her heels. It seemed to take ages for them to cross the yard and reach the two men who stood waiting for them.

"Reb, who—" Sarah Elizabeth said, then threw back her head and laughed.

Janet, too, was stunned to laughter when she recognized their felon. "Mr. Mooten? May I ask why you've caused all this trouble? You do realize you've given us quite a fright."

"Ground zero," Henry Mooten said simply. "See? I've been charting the activity all you folks have reported and I figured out this area right around here is the center of operations." He held out a notepad on which he'd drawn carefully detailed maps and calculations. In the darkness it was impossible to tell what purpose these drawings served.

"UFO Central." Reb snickered. "Right, Henry?"

Henry nodded. " 'At's right. The biggest events— like that Thorn woman's car being messed up, for instance—seem to start it. Like a hub. Right here. Now, you take these here other strange occurrences —cat having a whole litter born dead"—he pointed to his notes, which he seemed to feel would explain everything—"and gradually, gradually, as you go farther away from this here yard, out the spokes, so to speak, the events get fewer and farther between."

Reb winked at Sarah Elizabeth. "See?"

"But, Henry," Sarah Elizabeth said, "if a UFO had landed in my yard, I'm fairly sure I'd have noticed. Wouldn't it leave marks? You know, a burned area? Indentations in the ground?"

Janet was not able to determine from her tone whether Sarah Elizabeth was humoring the man or truly asking for information.

"Who's to say it landed?" Henry pointed out. "Maybe it just hovers. Maybe there's one great big mother ship that sends out little lightweight scouts. Maybe the doggone aliens can fly right on down here from their ship and walk away. *If*," he added in an ominous whisper, "they walk at all."

"Yes," Sarah Elizabeth agreed. "I see your point." Turning to Reb, she said, "Sorry. I guess we got you out of bed for nothing."

"I wasn't doing anything anyway," Reb said, and gave her another wink.

"And I'm sorry I put a scare into you," Henry apologized.

"We'll get over it," Sarah Elizabeth assured him. "But if you could just let me know in advance next time?"

"I'll do it," Henry quickly agreed. "Meanwhile, I'll just get comfortable out here for the night. I believe we'll have some activity real soon."

"You expect the UFO tonight, Mr. Mooten?" Janet asked.

"Maybe tonight, maybe tomorrow. You can count on me being here for the next little bit, though," he said. "I got a strong feeling they're comin' soon."

"You weren't, by chance, out here the night Mary Ann's car was vandalized?" Sarah Elizabeth asked. "Didn't see anything? Or anyone?"

"Sorry to say I wasn't," Henry admitted. "If you're looking for a suspect, I'd go first to them devil worshipers. Electromagnetic energy a UFO gives off can have a real negative effect on folks like that. They sorta work themselves into a frenzy, probably screw up their brains with drugs—makes 'em more susceptible to alien rays."

"Hadn't thought of that," Reb said.

Henry nodded, as if his point had been made. "Anyways, I'll be here every night till something happens."

"Any particular reason you think they'll come at night?" Reb asked.

"Less chance of being seen, I reckon. Ain't that the point of night patrol?" Henry took one last drag of his cigarette then fieldstripped it.

The kitchen had lost its warmth and comforting glow. With the lights turned on to avoid accidents, and with Sarah Elizabeth there for company, Janet found the room empty and unappealing. They were sharing hot cocoa, although Janet had lost her taste for it. She would have been glad to get to sleep herself, but Sarah Elizabeth had insisted that they have the cocoa to calm them down.

"Do you think," Janet asked her, "that it's a good idea to allow Mr. Mooten to continue his pursuit of flying saucers? It seems to me that he's received far too much encouragement already."

"I suppose someone has to be there to greet the aliens."

"Sarah Elizabeth, surely you do not believe that space aliens are visiting Earth."

Sarah Elizabeth shrugged. "Well, I've never seen an alien myself. But what does that prove?"

"It proves you're still sane," Janet said without compromise.

"Are you telling me that if you can't see it, it doesn't exist? How about love? Wind? Stuff like that there?"

"We can see the *results* of those things, Sarah Elizabeth. We cannot see the results of UFOs."

"Oh, I don't know. Maybe Henry has seen their landing pad. Maybe he's right about all these litters and satanists and whatnot being the result of UFO visitation. At any rate, Henry's happy and I don't mind him using the yard. I'm kind of flattered, actually, that he thinks aliens would land here. Do you think there'll be enough room in the yard?"

Janet swirled the last of her cocoa in the bottom of the cup, but did not drink it. "I understand why you humor him, of course," she went on. "He's a nice man and none of us wants to hurt his feelings. But it can't be good for him to go on this way. If nothing else, he could catch pneumonia standing outside all night."

"Oh, Henry's a tough old bird. Probably never been sick a day in his life. He's put a heck of a lot of effort into this, too. Going around, asking about strange happenings, then charting them all and figuring out the diameter and the circumference. I was terrible at that sort of thing in school. I'd ask Henry how he ever figured out we're at ground zero, but I'm afraid he might want to explain it." Sarah Elizabeth had opened a bag of marshmallows for her cocoa and now idly placed the sugary puffs on top of the table, forming first a circle, then a square.

"Still, I'd feel more comfortable knowing he's being taken care of. Does he have family?"

"Sure. Everybody's got one of those," Sarah Elizabeth said, dropping marshmallows into her hot cocoa. "It's a heavy responsibility—being ground zero. Maybe we should build a landing pad, just to let the aliens know we're willing to cooperate. Establish a meaningful dialogue. Intergalactic détente. Assuming, of course, that these aliens are from another galaxy. Could be they're from this one, I suppose."

"You've been awake too long," Janet said with concern.

Undaunted, Sarah Elizabeth continued. "We could take up donations for the construction of the landing pad, but what about the welcome sign? I wouldn't know what language to use. Maybe Henry knows." She snickered suddenly. "What do you suppose would happen if the aliens landed and demanded that Henry take them to his leader? Where would Henry go? Hey, what if they've been a bit off in their command of the language all these years, and what they really mean is 'Take us to the King'? What do you think they'd do when Henry told them Elvis is dead? On the other hand, maybe Elvis *isn't* dead and the aliens *know* that, and that's why—"

"Drink your cocoa," Janet ordered. "Then you're going to bed. You really must trim your schedule, Sarah Elizabeth. I believe your nerves are giving way."

Sarah Elizabeth giggled and nodded. "I think you're right. What fun! It's mah nerves! Ah'm havin' a nervous fit! Mah nerves just cain't take anymore! I'll finally fit into this family."

Janet would have sworn that Sarah Elizabeth's tone was tinged with bitterness, but no trace of it showed in her face. Studying her employer carefully, she could see fine lines around Sarah Elizabeth's eyes, and a deepening crease between her brows. She was beginning to look old and worn. Her face against the silk ruffle of her nightgown created a grotesque comparison. Whether she admitted it or not, Sarah Elizabeth was pushing herself beyond the limit and sooner or later she would find herself crashing face-first into a physical and emotional crisis.

"Maybe that's Mary Ann's problem," Janet mused aloud.

"Excuse me? You think she's affected by radiation from the UFOs? Of course! That explains a lot about this town, doesn't it?" Sarah Elizabeth raised her mug of cocoa in a mock salute. "To the aliens! They've made Jesus Creek what it is today."

Janet reached out and removed the cup from Sarah Elizabeth's hand, and set it carefully back on the table. "Sarah Elizabeth, you're giddy. I was merely thinking that the stress that has quite obviously affected your behavior may also explain Mary Ann's delusions. She is still recovering from the birth of little Eddie and the stress of moving away from family and familiar surroundings, after all. She knows almost no one in Jesus Creek and does not participate in hobbies, sports, or social activities. It seems to me that a woman who spends all her time cleaning, cooking, and caring for her family might experience the same stress that has clearly affected you. She is essentially a willing prisoner of her own home and family."

Sarah Elizabeth was leaning sideways in her chair, making faces at the puppy, who poked its nose cautiously around the laundry-room door. "Nonsense. Mary Ann is far more stressed than I am. *I* have never seen ghosts in the bedroom. I don't even believe in ghosts."

"I don't believe in demon possession, either. Yet the events Mary Ann has related to me are difficult to explain otherwise."

"Oh, yeah?" Sarah Elizabeth took a marshmallow from the open bag and tossed it at the puppy. "Like what?"

"In the beginning, there were sounds that she could not identify. According to a book borrowed from Delia Cannon, demon possession often begins with knocks, bangs, crashes, and so forth. Noises that have no discernible cause. Mary Ann, of course, was the only member of her family to hear these. Naturally it became upsetting as the disturbances continued and yet only Mary Ann seemed affected. She felt that Ted was not taking her fear seriously."

"Maybe she's picking up radio stations on her fillings. I heard about that happening once. Something to do with mercury—"

Ignoring her facetious manner, Janet went on. "There was also the intense sensation of being watched. On a few occasions she heard her name being called, or felt as if someone or something was beckoning to her. One night, I happened to glance out the window and I saw her looking out the door, as if searching for someone. She told me later that she'd felt *pulled* outside that night. Yet no other member of the family experienced this. According to Delia's book, demons often will select one household member. The fact that others in the same house are not experiencing the events will naturally cause division."

"Damn sure causes it around here," Sara Elizabeth agreed. "Mother Eliza has been chatting with the Civil War dead for ages and I can't help but think she's nuts. Silly me. I should have recognized it as demon possession right away." She tossed a handful of marshmallows in the air and attempted to catch them in her mouth. Her aim was bad and all of them landed on the floor.

"Perhaps you'd like to go up to bed now," Janet suggested.

"Nonsense. I'm dying to hear the rest of the story. What else is Mary Ann imagining?"

Reluctantly, Janet continued. "Her telephone rings, and yet no one is calling. All of these things taken together have strained her mental faculties greatly. Mary Ann's appearance is quite dramatically changed. Have you seen her lately?"

"You do realize," Sarah Elizabeth pointed out, with sudden clarity, "that all these tales are purely subjective. Do you really want to take her word for it? You don't believe in Henry's UFOs, so why do you believe Mary Ann's tales of supernatural horror? Mary Ann could well be looking for attention. She might be just a little bit bonkers. She could have a physical problem that needs medical attention. Or maybe the Thorns are just another dysfunctional family. Goodness knows, there's plenty of us in the world."

Janet could not argue with anything Sarah Elizabeth had just said. In fact, she'd considered it all herself and come to the conclusion that what Mary Ann needed was not an exorcist, but a therapist. Still, Mary Ann's conviction was strong and Janet could not shake her initial opinion of the woman— that Mary Ann was a sensible, sturdy, down-to-earth person who would not allow herself to be spooked by an occasional bump in the night.

"Her tires *were* slashed," Janet pointed out. "And I have seen deep scratches on her throat and shoulder, inflicted, she says, during the night while she slept. Wouldn't you think that a human hand causing those injuries would have gotten her attention?"

"I'd think so, yes. I've been wrong before, though. It's also possible that she's lying. Ask some of our battered women where they got their black eyes. They'll tell you they ran into doors. Never fails." Finishing the last of her cocoa, Sarah Elizabeth rose from her chair and moved slowly toward the puppy. "Come here, you little furball," she said softly. "Come here and I'll pat your fuzzy head."

The puppy cowered, but did not back away.

"You're wasting your time," Janet told her. "I have tried and tried to establish friendship, but that animal simply will not have it. After we've fed it and talked to it and given it a lovely home, it shows no appreciation at all. I can't understand it."

"Puppy's behavior seems irrational to us because we expect a certain response to certain actions. We think if we care for her, she'll love us back. But the critter's been trained to fear humans. She knows that nothing is guaranteed, especially human behavior. Her earliest memory is probably of being kicked in the teeth. Actually, *we're* irrational to expect any behavior other than this."

"But after days and days of receiving tender loving care, I should think—"

"Old terrors never die," Sarah Elizabeth said. "They just hide in the closet and jump out at you when you least expect it." She had taken one step too many, and the puppy scurried back into the shadows of the laundry room. "Well, so much for that. We'd better get to bed. At least we can sleep well tonight, knowing that Henry is on guard duty."

Janet rose from her chair, gathered both mugs, and rinsed them at the sink. "I'm not at all sure that I am comforted by the knowledge. Does he plan to spend every night in the yard?"

"Probably just until he finds a new obsession," Sarah Elizabeth said. "Or spots a UFO. Henry's harmless, though. And I don't mind knowing that someone's keeping an eye on this place. With all the stray batterers wandering about, I'm grateful there's someone on our side. Even Henry."

"I'll be sure to mention this to Mary Ann tomorrow. In her current state of agitation, she might spot Henry in the yard and take leave of her senses altogether."

"Maybe she could join up with him," Sarah Elizabeth suggested. "A hobby could be good for her. Get her mind off her troubles. Better yet, we could have our battered women form their own UFO-watch club. They're all as neurotic as Mary Ann anyway. Might as well put that to good use."

It was a connection that Janet would never have made on her own. Mary Ann, battered women. Having observed the handful of women who'd sought shelter in Sarah Elizabeth's house, and having heard the tales of many more who'd come through SAN's doors in the past, Janet had already begun to notice similarities in them. It was possible, she now realized, that Mary Ann's symptoms were indeed of the type she'd found in Missy and Melinda. Denial of the obvious threat, a refusal to seek help even when it was readily available, isolating themselves in a house or a room, fabricating outlandish stories to explain their injuries—there could be many more connections.

Try as she might, though, Janet could not imagine Ted Thorn abusing his wife. He'd brought her flowers, she recalled, and seemed totally devoted, proud of Mary Ann's devotion to her home and family. He was a successful professional, with a healthy income and good education. To be thorough, Janet would investigate the possibility, but it seemed extremely unlikely that domestic violence was a factor in Mary Ann's situation.

Sarah Elizabeth had gone upstairs with the half-full bag of marshmallows clutched in her hand. "And if I dream I'm eating my pillow—" she said, and giggled.

With her employer presumably tucked in for the night, Janet felt as if she'd earned her sleep. The house was eerily silent for a change as she made her way up the staircase on tiptoe.

Before going to bed, Janet decided to look in on Leesha and Katrina sleeping in one of the extra rooms.

The room was small but freshly painted in cheerful shades of rose and moss green. Twin beds had been tucked in on either side of a dresser, and the room could at least boast a large window that allowed sunlight to brighten it in the daytime.

Katrina was curled into a ball, arms tightly clutching a ragged bear she'd brought from home. Awake, the child often grated on Janet's nerves. She was rowdy and rambunctious, demanding and even shrill at times. But sound asleep, with her thumb just falling out of her mouth, Katrina seemed the picture of innocence and purity.

Leesha, however, was on her side, face turned to the wall and sobbing quite audibly. When Janet called her name, Leesha's sobbing stopped abruptly. Janet waited, sure that Leesha had heard her, but the girl did not respond. It was obvious that she did not want company or consolation, as much as she might need both. Leesha's determination to be an independent young lady was admirable, but she would have to learn soon that everyone, at some time, is vulnerable. Reluctantly, Janet chose to respect her privacy and softly closed the door.

It was no wonder that the girl was crying herself to sleep, Janet realized, when she remembered that Melinda's preliminary hearing was set for the next day. While the hearing was only to determine whether there was probable cause to go to trial, Janet was sure that Melinda would not walk away a free woman. Reb had not been able or willing to discuss the case with Sarah Elizabeth or any one else, but rumor spreads quickly in a small town.

Melinda had motive. Everyone knew that. James Forrest's gun was missing and Melinda surely would have had access to it. That gave her the means to kill him. And opportunity? If anyone else had been near the Forrest house the day of the murder, it had not been mentioned.

Leesha probably knew the truth and would undoubtedly be called to testify at some point. If she'd witnessed the murder, she would have to choose between protecting her mother and perjuring herself. It would have been remarkable, in fact, if Leesha slept at all.

For all the times Janet had wished to exchange her own mother for another one, she now apologized. While her mother might be eccentric and irresponsible, immature and irritating, at least she had never committed murder in front of her daughter.

In her own bed, snuggled under heavy quilts, Janet found that she could sleep no better than Leesha. Henry Mooten's presence was a deterrent only to corporeal prowlers. Janet's sleeplessness was caused by something intangible and far more disturbing.

Her friend Mary Ann was suffering from a form of terrorism, either real or imagined. It might be caused by evil spirits, unhappy and somehow blaming Mary Ann. In that case, Janet knew of no way to end her suffering, short of full exorcism, and even that was uncertain. Or Mary Ann might have succumbed to an insidious form of madness that spread itself from person to person and that had *already* begun creeping through the Leach household. Through all of Jesus Creek, perhaps, and Janet was wholly serious this time when she considered the behavior of most of the residents she'd met. They were unique, surely eccentric, and sometimes entertaining. But if she looked at them objectively, would she find that Henry, and Eliza Leach, and even Sarah Elizabeth suffered from a documented illness that passed itself off as colorful personality?

And now there was the newly recognized possibility that Mary Ann was a battered woman. The scratches that she claimed had appeared during the night—might they be evidence of a brutal attack by her husband? Did she carry other scars? Bruises, inflicted on her body in places a casual acquaintance would never see?

It was almost impossible to believe, but Janet knew that the impossible was often nothing more than ignorance of the subject. Sarah Elizabeth had chided her for refusing to believe in UFOs simply because she had never seen one. It was easy to believe that Mary Ann bore no bruises, since Janet had never seen them. But it wasn't something Mary Ann would display, was it? Evidence of her husband's brutality would be kept hidden out of fear and humiliation.

Sarah Elizabeth had given her the statistics—one in four homes harbored domestic violence. Janet had not believed the numbers, had not believed this crime was so prevalent. She had not seen it. She had not looked, she admitted to herself, and it was unlikely that any of her neighbors would invite her over to watch while it happened.

At any rate, it would do no harm to look a little closer at her friend. Janet would almost welcome a discovery of domestic violence. That, at least, was a problem for which there was a solution.

CHAPTER

9

THE ANGELA COUNTY COURTHOUSE WAS AT least one hundred years old. Solid and dignified, it stood in the center of the Jesus Creek court square, surrounded by benches and stone monuments and, currently, a small crowd of shoppers, court watchers, and checkers players.

As the entire Leach household (minus Eliza) climbed the south steps, Janet felt as if they were under scrutiny by all the casual passersby. Leesha and Katrina would, by now, be known to everyone in town as the children of a woman accused of murdering her husband. It would easily be concluded that Janet and Sarah Elizabeth and even little Ariel were also connected to the Forrest family. Janet chided herself for feeling a trace of embarrassment.

Sarah Elizabeth was doubly burdened this morning. Shortly before they'd left for the courthouse, they had received news of Karen, the woman who'd been recently hospitalized by her husband's attack. She had died during the night. It was no comfort to Sarah Elizabeth that the husband would now be charged with murder. "A lot of good that does Kar-

147

en," she'd remarked bitterly. "Or any of the other women out there. Knowing that the law won't stop him until he kills her isn't comforting or reasonable, is it?"

"In fairness," Janet had reminded her, "Karen might have sought help before the abuse escalated to this point."

"Yes," Sarah Elizabeth had agreed. "Half the battle is convincing women that the men they love are dangerous. Every single one thinks she's different, that her man would never really hurt her." She shook her head in resignation. "I think the chances of women worldwide coming to their senses are pretty slim."

Sitting in the courtroom with the children sandwiched between herself and Sarah Elizabeth, Janet surreptitiously watched the other courtroom observers. They all seemed bored, she thought, unless what passed for apathy was really extreme tension. Sarah Elizabeth's feelings were written plainly on her tight face. It might as well be *her* life up for grabs in this courtroom, Janet thought. One would think Sarah Elizabeth would have adjusted to reality by now, after so much time working with battered women. Indeed, there were moments when Janet had seen her hang up the hotline and laughingly report, "There's one who won't get out until she's dead." Her attitude at those times seemed heartless, but then she would turn around and cry all morning over someone like Karen who'd passed briefly through her life and disappeared.

At the front of the room, Melinda sat between her court-appointed attorney and his assistant. Having been told by Sarah Elizabeth that Devereaux Maddox was a brilliant attorney, known to fight tooth and nail for even his indigent clients, Janet was surprised by his appearance. She had expected a powerfully built, charismatic man. What she saw instead was a small, neat, fair-haired man, who looked to her like a timid mouse. He shuffled frantically through the stack of papers in front of him until his unflappable assistant plucked one from the pile and handed it to him without a word.

Janet was not comfortable with having Leesha and Katrina in court to see their mother in her near-catatonic state. But Leesha had insisted, and with such intensity that it was clear she would not stay away. Since both Sarah Elizabeth and Janet were equally determined to attend, there had been no choice but to bring along the girls as well.

With the judge seated and appropriate announcements set forth, the prosecution's first witness began his testimony.

Reb Gassler did not seem in the least uncomfortable, even though he could clearly see Sarah Elizabeth watching. Janet admired him for maintaining his composure, knowing as she did that his sympathy lay with Melinda.

"Chief Gassler," the prosecutor began, "how did you become involved in the investigation of James Forrest's murder?"

It seemed to Janet that the prosecutor was not terribly interested in the answer to his question. It occurred to her that he might be going through the motions only because that was his job and not because he believed he had any real evidence against Melinda.

"I received a radio transmission from my dispatcher informing me that Tad Hopkins had called the station to report a shooting at Forrest's address," Reb explained. "I drove immediately to the address to investigate."

"And what did you find upon your arrival?"

Reb pulled a small notepad from his shirt pocket and flipped it open. "Mr. Hopkins met me in the front yard of the home. He reported that he had ar-

rived at around six-thirty P.M., found Mr. Forrest in
the floor and obviously injured, then called 911 for
help. When I arrived, I pronounced Forrest dead."

"Was anyone else on the scene at that time,
Chief?"

"Two ambulance attendants were waiting to load
the body into the ambulance."

"Were there any lights on in the house?"

Janet could not imagine why lights were important. As she understood it, the purpose of this hearing was to determine probable cause, not wasteful
use of electricity.

"Were the doors to the house locked, Chief?"

Reb shook his head, then remembered that the
court reporter required a verbal response. "No, sir.
The front door was wide open when I got there. Mr.
Hopkins told me he'd found it that way when he arrived. I checked and found the back inner door
open and the screen door slightly ajar."

Reb and the prosecutor went on to discuss blood-
stains and bullet fragments at great length. Janet
felt it would have been a speedier processing if Reb
had been allowed to tell his story without interrup-
tion. Instead, the prosecutor asked one question in
language so simple Ariel could have understood it,
asked the same question in two or three different
ways, and circled each answer like a buzzard circling a dying dog.

"Did you perform a gunshot residue test on Mrs.
Forrest, Chief?"

"Yes," Reb answered, "but the results have not
yet been released from the crime lab."

"Did you find a .357 Magnum inside the house?"

"No," Reb said, "only an empty Uncle Mike's hol-
ster."

The prosecutor seemed genuinely confused. "You
lost me there."

Janet suspected this knowledge pleased Reb im-

mensely, given that his response was clearly conde-
scending. "It's a name brand for a black nylon hol-
ster, sort of inexpensive."

Moving on, the prosecutor asked about the exact
position of the body.

"He was on his back, sprawled out in the living-
room floor with his head just in the doorway to the
kitchen," Reb said. His eyes closed almost imper-
ceptibly, as if he wanted to shut out the sight of
James Forrest's corpse. "His arms and legs were
spread-eagle, with his palms up."

The prosecutor passed his witness to Maddox,
who rose and transformed himself instantly into
the legendary figure Janet had been led to expect.
He could have been a wizard, magically changing
from mouse to lion, the way his presence suddenly
and completely filled the courtroom. No one dared
to cough or shuffle while he spoke, nor would they
dare to give less than their full attention to what
he had to say.

"Chief, have you spoken to Mrs. Melinda Forrest
about her husband's death?"

"I spoke with her at the hospital shortly after the
body was discovered." Reb glanced at Melinda, looking more sympathetic than a prosecution witness
should.

"Do you know why Mrs. Forrest was in the hospital that night?"

Reb nodded. "She had been treated in the emergency room for a broken wrist and some bruises."

"Would that have been her right or left wrist,
Chief?"

"I believe it was her left one."

"And do you know whether Mrs. Forrest is right-
or left-handed?"

"No, sir, I don't."

"And did she tell you how her wrist was broken?"

Maddox spoke softly, while still managing to suggest that this question was of extreme importance.

"She said it was an accident."

"Aha." Maddox seemed satisfied with the answer. "And do you know the nature of that accident?"

"Mrs. Forrest's daughter informed me that Mr. Forrest had broken the arm."

Nodding slightly, Maddox moved behind his table and glanced at a paper there. "Chief Gassler, did you question Mr. Tad Hopkins about his recent altercation with James Forrest?"

For the first time in his testimony Reb seemed unsure of himself. "I wasn't aware there'd been one," he said.

"Who, besides Tad Hopkins, did you interview on the scene?"

"No one else on the scene. I talked to some of the neighbors, but they all live too far away to have seen anything at the Forrest house."

Maddox mulled this over for a minute, then asked, "Did any of them hear a gunshot?"

"Nobody said so." Rob delivered the last with a shake of his head that suggested he was sorry he could not provide some bit of information to the defense attorney.

"Did they mention having seen any cars pulling into or out of the Forrest driveway?"

"No, sir," Reb answered.

"None of the neighbors saw Mrs. Forrest driving to the hospital?"

"Not as far as I know."

"And not a single neighbor saw Tad Hopkins pull into the Forrest driveway?"

"No, sir," Reb repeated.

"They also did not see any other vehicles in the area?"

"No, sir."

It would have been surprising, Janet thought, if the neighbors *had* seen anything. Normal activity in one's own neighborhood went unnoticed. Except for a gunshot and a murder, nothing had been out of place that day. What was it, she wondered, that Maddox hoped to find?

"As I understand it," Maddox continued, "the medical examiner says James Forrest died right about six-thirty P.M."

"Yes, sir. Tad Hopkins arrived just about that time and the victim actually died while Mr. Hopkins was on the phone calling 911. Medical examiner says Forrest could have been shot anywhere from twenty to forty minutes earlier."

Twenty to forty minutes allowed more than enough time for someone to have come in after Melinda left, Janet realized. Unfortunately it also meant that Melinda could have shot him and still had enough time to get to the hospital by six-twelve P.M., the time emergency-room records showed she'd been admitted.

Having walked into the courthouse earlier that morning expecting the brilliant Mr. Maddox to exonerate Melinda Forrest, Janet found herself growing more and more depressed. Nothing she'd heard sounded promising for Melinda's case. Janet thought a better strategy might have been to have Melinda admit to shooting her husband, using self-defense as an excuse.

If the purpose of this hearing had been to prove probable cause, the state had succeeded admirably. At this point, Janet thought the best Melinda could hope for was a manslaughter conviction.

While Sarah Elizabeth took the girls to Eloise's Diner for lunch, Janet decided to use her free time for investigation. She strolled down the sidewalk on Morning Glory Way, considering and rejecting ways to introduce the subject of Mary Ann's possible victim status to Delia Cannon. At last she decided that discretion must prevail. She would not mention Mary Ann at all. Instead, she would allow herself a tiny white lie and tell Delia that she was thinking of becoming a SAN volunteer. Given the amount of time she'd already spent listening to tales of woe, counseling Melinda, and baby-sitting the offspring of victims, Janet felt the organization owed her a fib or two.

Delighted to find Delia at home, Janet was more than glad to accept her invitation to share a cup of herb tea. "I grew the camomile myself," Delia said with a touch of pride. "And I throw in a handful of peppermint leaves, too. Wonderful for indigestion or sleeplessness. Would you like it straight or with honey?"

"Straight, please," Janet told her, thinking that a dab of honey probably would not hide the taste of the weeds anyway. Janet's mother had taken to herbal teas early in Janet's life and, on those rare occasions when she returned home, had insisted that Janet try them all. Unfortunately, by the time the tea had been transported in her mother's duffel bag along with a mass of incense, it all smelled equally repulsive. To this day, Janet could not tell the difference between the scent of camomile and the scent of sandalwood.

"How'd the hearing go?" Delia wanted to know.

"Normally, I suppose," Janet told her. "I've never witnessed one before. It was discouraging, in that none of the information given clears Melinda, or even casts doubt on her guilt."

"Don't tell Sarah Elizabeth," Delia warned. "I wouldn't want to upset her. But you can count on Melinda being convicted of manslaughter at the very least."

"Surely not!" Janet was more than a little

surprised by Delia's pessimism. "Self-defense is surely—"

"Self-defense requires two equally matched opponents or at least the threat of severe injury. Melinda's husband wasn't armed when she shot him. They haven't even found *one* gun, much less a second that he might have been using."

"But she hasn't admitted shooting him," Janet said with alarm. What *had* become of the rational, fair-minded Delia Cannon she'd met before?

"Well, of course not. And personally I'm ready to testify that she was here with me the whole time. Let's face it, the man needed killing." Delia set the tea in front of Janet and took a sip of her own. "On the other hand, murder is murder. We can't turn people loose—not even battered women—just because killing someone seemed like a good idea at the time."

"But the provocation—" Janet protested.

"Doesn't justify the crime. Look, I know the legal system is unfair to these women. Before she fights back, she's supposed to make every effort to leave the scene. Why *should* she? And self-defense means meeting force with equal force and nothing more, but that puts a ninety-five-pound woman at a serious disadvantage when a two-hundred-pound man is armed with only his fists. And I can't tell you how many times we've had a cop or even a judge tell one of our battered women to go home, behave herself, and stop asking for it. But that doesn't mean she has to resort to a shotgun. That's what SAN is for."

Janet understood the logic of Delia's argument, but felt that more than fair play had to be considered. "Still, if what I've heard from all of you is true, most of these women are actually killed after they leave the abusers."

Delia nodded agreement. "Absolutely. But murder isn't the answer." She finished the last of her tea in a gulp and pounded the cup down on the table. "Here," she said, reaching across the table. "Give me your cup and I'll pour it down the sink."

"Oh, it's quite good. Really," Janet insisted. She *had* given herself permission to fib.

"Yes, it is," Delia agreed. "But you have that same look on your face I've seen on Roger's so often. Why don't I get you some coffee? Regular coffee, lots of caffeine."

"No, please don't bother. I seem to be swimming in coffee lately. I came by today, in fact, to get information. About battered women." Janet wondered if she should explain that *she*, of course, was not a victim of violence, but surely Delia could see that. "I've been thinking of volunteering," she added quickly, just in case Delia couldn't. "There are so many questions to ask, though. Suppose you get a call on the hotline from a crackpot. There must be plenty of them out there. How do you recognize a fraud?"

Delia pondered the question while making herself another cup of the vile herb tea. It seemed to Janet that the possibility had never occurred to her before. At last she returned to the table, cup in hand, and replied, "I guess because a domestic violence hotline isn't something people would call for a lark. Hell, real victims don't like to admit it. Calling the hotline is a last-ditch effort. These women insist on telling us how wonderful their husbands are."

"Battered women don't know they're battered." Janet nodded.

"Exactly," Delia said. "Define battering. Your definition may not match mine. One woman doesn't think she's battered because he's never hit her with his fist, only slapped her around. Another thinks *she's* not battered because he only uses his fists, not a big stick."

"But if a woman is being regularly slapped, for instance, and doesn't realize she's a victim of abuse, how can an outsider hope to determine the truth?"

Delia shrugged. "Instinct is useful. Of course, there are the standard symptoms of abuse: separation from friends and family, so that she has no support system; she's kept under surveillance, by him or his family or friends; he exhibits jealous rages, with or without cause; he keeps her hungry or exhausted or both; he keeps her dependent on him for drugs or money or whatever."

Janet held up her hand to stop the flow of information. "All this should be glaringly obvious, then. Why doesn't someone notice and step in to help?"

"Well, it *sounds* obvious. But most batterers are also master manipulators. Look, he doesn't hide the money and tell her he's doing it to keep her dependent. He tells her she doesn't know how to handle money, or that there just isn't any money. It's all very subtle, really. And she is slowly, over a period of time, trained to believe it. Just as she's trained to believe that she deserves to be beaten, to be punished for her inferiority."

"You keep calling the victims *she*," Janet pointed out. "Aren't men ever beaten by their wives?"

"Oh, sure," Delia told her. "Have you ever met a man who'd call the hotline and admit that the little woman punched his lights out? That he can't control his wife? Good heavens, what would his friends say?"

"I don't know," Janet admitted. "I suppose they'd say he ought to hit her back."

Delia gave her an approving smile. "Which doesn't solve a thing, does it?"

* * *

Janet joined the others at Eloise's in time to catch them paying for the meal.

The afternoon sky threatened rain, but Sarah Elizabeth insisted that Janet and the children take her car for the drive home. It would have been less trouble, Janet realized, for them to walk, given the time and energy involved in strapping Ariel and Katrina into their seats. But she chose not to argue. The morning's testimony seemed to have taken quite a toll on Sarah Elizabeth, who looked even more depressed than Janet felt.

Opting to skip the afternoon session, Leesha announced her intention to walk over to the Medical Center and collect her mother's car at long last.

"Don't forget the keys!" Katrina chirped from her backseat perch.

"Got 'em," Leesha said absently, digging through her shoulder bag for the car keys. "I'll be right behind you," she told Janet, and headed off on foot toward the Medical Center.

Indeed, by the time Janet had pulled the massive Buick out of its parking space and circled around the courthouse, Leesha was pulling up behind her. They arrived at the Leach house together, with Leesha parking her car half on, half off the sidewalk in front of the house.

They could not miss the boat. It stood in the Thorns' driveway, a bright metallic blue, glinting in the midday sun. Ted was slowly circling the boat, as if checking to see that all the parts were there. Mary Ann stood nearby, looking somewhat stunned, as if perhaps the boat had been dropped in her yard unexpectedly.

"Leesha, take Katrina in the house and try to get her down for a nap," Janet said as she removed Ariel from the child-safety seat. "I'm going next door for a few minutes." Lifting Ariel free of the car, she wrapped a blanket around the child and walked across the yard.

"How wonderful!" she said enthusiastically. "A boat is ideal for family outings. Picnics on the shore, waterskiing—"

"Whoa!" Ted said with a laugh. "This is a fishing boat, not a recreational vehicle. In a few years I guess Eddie will go out with me. But what would Mary Ann do? Imagine her trying to get a fish off the line."

Mary Ann smiled in agreement. "Besides," she added, as if defending Ted's statement, "I can't swim. I'm scared to death of water."

Janet, who had quite enjoyed fishing throughout her childhood, was certain that Mary Ann would get the hang of it in no time . . . if she tried. She resolved to keep that opinion to herself for the time being. Ted obviously did not want to share his hobby. In the first place, Janet understood the need for solitude that he might find in a day of bass fishing. More than that, though, her silence was ensured by her fear that Mary Ann was a victim of physical assault. Janet did not want to argue with Ted, angering him and causing him to vent that anger on his wife.

"Well," she said at last, "it's lovely. My grandfather has a boat, but nothing like this. An old, battered tub, really." Now, why did she have to say *battered*? "I'm sure you'll have many hours of pleasure from it."

Ted, apparently captivated by the exquisite beauty of his new possession, seemed not to have heard her. Mary Ann answered in his stead. "Ted's wanted a boat for ages. He just loves to fish. Don't you, dear?"

"Long as I catch something," Ted agreed. "And as long as you don't burn it after I bring it home."

Mary Ann shrugged. "I don't know what my

problem is," she said to Janet. "I never can cook fish right."

"It's not limited to fish," Ted reminded her. "You have trouble with beef and pork and chicken—"

"Yeah." Mary Ann laughed. "Food in general."

Janet watched the exchange silently, trying to determine if Mary Ann felt threatened by her husband's presence. The slacks and light jacket she wore covered her body, so that Janet could not have seen bruises if they'd been there. She could not, however, detect tension between the Thorns, nor did Mary Ann seem frightened or nervous. Well, no more nervous than usual these last few weeks.

"I won't keep you from enjoying your new purchase," she said. "We've just returned from the hearing for Melinda Forrest and I want to get the girls calmed as quickly as I can."

"That's such a sad case," Mary Ann said. "I hear there's no family. What will happen to those kids when their mother's in prison?"

"One hopes their mother will be freed," Janet pointed out. "So that the family can be reunited. Until then, the girls will continue to stay with us."

"You'd think that woman would have thought about her kids before she shot her husband," Ted said. "Didn't it occur to her that she'd be locked up? I guess she thought she could get away with it, though. They always do."

"Melinda has not admitted to committing the murder," Janet reminded him. "But if she did shoot him, I'm sure she felt it was the only way to protect herself. You may not be aware of the brutal treatment she's received in the past."

"Oh, I've read about it in the paper. And I sure think he *should* have been shot. After all, a man who beats his wife isn't much of a man, is he? I'm just saying she should have left him. Gotten a divorce. Whatever. Killing the man was a big mistake and now her kids have to pay for it."

Janet agreed that murder was not the best solution to Melinda Forrest's domestic problems. However, after learning of Karen's death this morning, and hearing those horror stories of legal injustice from Delia Cannon, she wondered if Melinda had really had an acceptable choice.

"Well, she won't come down and she doesn't want food brought up to her." Sara Elizabeth flopped into a kitchen chair, then leaned forward to take Ariel from Janet.

"She's spitting out her oatmeal," Janet said, and handed Sarah Elizabeth the towel she'd been using to wipe cereal from Ariel's chin. "I hope Mrs. Leach isn't ill. A virus, maybe?"

Sarah Elizabeth fed her daughter another spoonful of cereal, which the child promptly pushed out with her tongue. "Could be. Or more likely, she's just being stubborn."

Janet thought it equally likely that Eliza Leach could feel the strain in the house and hoped to avoid it by staying in her room. Dinner had been a dismal affair for them all. Leesha sniffed her way through it, reprimanding Katrina more than once and finally pushing her plate away untouched. Sarah Elizabeth had had no more appetite than Leesha. For that matter, neither had Janet. None of them could overcome the sense of disappointment that the preliminary hearing had brought.

"If Mrs. Leach isn't down for breakfast tomorrow, I'll look in on her. I had planned to take the children for a visit next door, but if you think I should stay here—"

"No, by all means, go visiting. Mother Eliza will be fine."

"All the same, I'll make a point of checking on

her throughout the day." Janet leaned slightly forward and added, "I intend to keep a close eye on Mary Ann, too."

Sarah Elizabeth raised an eyebrow. "Really? What's up?"

With a sigh, Janet eased into explanation. "I've been concerned," she began, "I hope without cause. You're aware that Mary Ann has been plagued by strange and frightening occurrences."

"Her ghosts." Sarah Elizabeth nodded.

"As I consider other possibilities, I find that symptoms of possession by a supernatural entity are quite similar to symptoms of a number of physical ailments. I would prefer to have a physician's report on the state of Mary Ann's health. But she refuses to go for a checkup—she says it's too expensive. I can't believe their financial status is that desperate, given that Ted just bought what must have been a very expensive boat."

"I saw that in their driveway," Sarah Elizabeth said. "Of course, he might have bought it used. Still, it would have cost more than a doctor's visit."

Janet nodded agreement. "At any rate, Mary Ann refuses to admit that she may have health problems. I've also considered depression. She seldom leaves her house. You may have noticed that her personal grooming lacks enthusiasm lately."

"Wouldn't surprise me a bit. You know," Sarah Elizabeth said, "you might talk to Ted about this. He'd have a better idea of her mental and physical condition than we could guess at."

"I have considered that, of course. But at this point, I'm afraid I suspect that he may be the cause of the problem."

"Oh, no," Sarah Elizabeth said with a heavy sigh. "You know, I live in absolute fear of hearing a friend's voice on the hotline. It's all I can do to maintain an objective attitude anyway."

Janet stopped, unsure if Sarah Elizabeth meant that she did not want to hear the rest of the story.

But Sarah Elizabeth herself encouraged further conversation. "What have you noticed?" she asked. "Bruises? Has she said anything about being slapped or—"

"No, not at all. Both she and Ted express revulsion at the idea of domestic violence. Ted has even said to me that he feels James Forrest deserved exactly what he got. And I hope to find that I've jumped to an entirely erroneous conclusion. But I felt it necessary to explore all the possibilities."

"Good point," Sarah Elizabeth said. "So what have you got?"

"I borrowed a book from Delia Cannon. A book about demonic possession."

"I thought you'd ruled that out," Sarah Elizabeth said.

"Of course I have. But the information, if accurate, proved interesting from another standpoint. It states that there are four stages of possession. The first is infestation, during which the spirit commits acts that are nuisances, but not overtly dangerous. Tapping, whistling, turning lights on and off. This is designed to merely get the attention of the victim, who then begins casting about for a logical explanation."

"Okay," Sarah Elizabeth said. "And *is* there a logical explanation in Mary Ann's case?"

"That is less important than the tension caused by these actions. Particularly when only one member of the household is exposed. The key word, of course, is tension. Isn't that an early part of the domestic violence cycle?"

"Yes, it is," Sarah Elizabeth admitted. "But tension is everywhere. I don't think it's all caused by domestic violence or ghosts."

"Stage Two." Janet held up two fingers. "Oppression. The spirit steps up the attack, continuing to knock and tap, but adding more destructive acts, such as breaking objects in the house. The point here is to let the victim know that nothing she does makes any difference. She cannot make it go away and she is powerless to stop it."

"Just as the battered woman is powerless to stop assaults on herself. She can't control his behavior." Sarah Elizabeth had made the connection. "Is there more?"

"Stage Three is possession, during which the spirit—"

"Takes control of the victim," Sarah Elizabeth finished. "Monitoring her phone calls, conversations, funds. Keeping her constantly under surveillance by pretending to take an active interest in her life. Calling and hanging up, just to make sure she's home."

"Perhaps forcing her to remain in her prison by disabling her car?" Janet asked.

"And naturally she's too exhausted to fight back anymore, because the tension and low-level terrorism won't allow her to rest." Sarah Elizabeth leaned back in her chair and propped Ariel on the shoulder. "There's a demon in the house. We've just misidentified the demon."

Janet had hoped Sarah Elizabeth would call her foolish, would point out the inconsistencies, not bolster her theory. If she had pooh-poohed Janet's idea, Janet would have gladly dropped it and begun searching for a less frightening cause. Now she feared she had no choice but to accept Mary Ann as a battered woman and herself as the helpless friend, uncertain how to proceed.

"What's the next stage?" Sarah Elizabeth asked.

Janet took a deep breath before answering. "Death."

DEATH

C H A P T E R

10

MOST RESIDENTS OF JESUS CREEK WERE blissfully unaware that Karen was dead, that Melinda was imprisoned, or that Janet Ayres was obsessed with discovering a solution to Mary Ann's problems.

Leesha was dressed and ready for school when she came downstairs. It amazed Janet that the girl was able to keep up her studies, while playing mother to little Katrina and worrying about Melinda. Leesha was turning out to be a strong and determined young woman. A survivor. Janet sincerely wished that survival had not been necessary.

"Katrina needs chores to do," Leesha announced, pouring out a bowl of cereal for her little sister. "She's got way too much energy, and besides, she's old enough to start taking responsibility."

"A good idea," Janet agreed. "What do you suggest?"

"For starters, she ought to make the bed. And pick up all her toys before bedtime." Leesha sat down at the table, but ignored the breakfast she'd prepared for herself. "It wouldn't hurt to have her fill the dog's bowl, either, but I'm afraid she might scare the poor little thing and then it would never come out from behind the washer."

As if to prove her older sister right, Katrina slapped her spoon down in the cereal bowl and sent milk flying across the table.

"And she can clean that up," Leesha added. "Find a dishtowel, Katrina, and wipe up the mess."

"You do it," Katrina said with an impish grin.

"No." Leesha was calm but firm. She remained in her seat and stared at the little girl.

Katrina turned her attention to the cereal still in her bowl, as if completely unaware of Leesha's stare.

"Katrina, I had hoped we might visit with Eddie next door," Janet sad. "But we can't enjoy ourselves until our work at home is finished. Either you clean the table or stay home."

"I'll stay home," Katrina said, and continued eating.

"Katrina," Sarah Elizabeth snapped. "Clean that up now!"

Her tone and volume got the child's attention, as well as Janet's. It was uncharacteristic of Sarah Elizabeth to be short-tempered, especially with someone as vulnerable as Katrina was now. Still, Sarah Elizabeth had gotten action. Within seconds, the table was wiped clean and Katrina was sullenly eating her breakfast.

Neither Janet nor Leesha commented, but both glanced warily at Sarah Elizabeth as she snatched up her jacket and purse and gave Ariel a quick kiss. "I'll be home as soon as I can tonight," she said tersely, and stalked out of the room.

"I'm sorry," Leesha said when she was gone. "I know having us here is getting on her nerves."

"A great many things are getting on her nerves," Janet promised. "You certainly are not to blame."

"Well, anyway. We can't stay here forever. I don't know what we're going to do if Mom doesn't get out soon." Leesha pushed her uneaten breakfast away from her. "I'll probably have to get a job. I could make enough to pay rent on a little place."

"No, you could not." Janet did not believe that now was the time for optimistic fantasy. "Sarah Elizabeth is perfectly happy to have you remain here. Certainly that's the best place for you at the moment. Once your mother is free—"

"And when will that be?" Leesha demanded. "You heard all that stuff they said in court yesterday. There's no way she can make bail. She was in the hospital when he died and I was there with her, but nobody believes me."

"I don't know, Leesha." Janet reached over and patted the girl's shoulder. "Unless Mr. Maddox can pinpoint the time of the shooting, it will be difficult to prove that your mother could not have done it. But he seems a capable attorney. If your mother is innocent—"

"She *is* innocent.. She didn't kill anybody. You've seen her, Janet. If she could kill somebody, don't you think she'd have done it years ago? She didn't *like* the way he treated us!" Leesha's voice was choked with sobs. "She's just one of those people. She wants everything to be quiet and peaceful and she wants everybody to be happy. And if something goes wrong, she tries to ignore it and hopes it'll go away."

"I know you love your mother very much. We must believe that justice will be served and that she will be home again soon."

"If justice was going to be served," Leesha said, "it would have happened a long time ago. If life

was going to be fair, she never would have wound
up married to *him*."

Janet found that she had no convincing argument against this reasoning. Obviously Melinda
was going to suffer through a difficult few months
while awaiting trial. It would be unrealistic to expect a jury to acquit her of murder simply because
she'd suffered in the past.

If only someone had seen an out-of-place car near
the Forrest house, Janet thought, there might be
hope. If somehow it could be proved that James
Forrest had been shot just minutes before Tad
Hopkins arrived, instead of a half hour or more
earlier, Melinda certainly would be released. She
knew that Reb and his officers were actively
searching for the gun that had killed Forrest, but
did not have a reasonable expectation of finding it.

There was still the slim possibility that Devereaux
Maddox had a trump card—some small but vital
piece of information that would turn the case around
when presented to a jury. Janet realized she was
clutching at straws, trying to turn a small-town lawyer into Perry Mason with a drawl.

She had known the Forrest family for such a
short time and yet had become so deeply involved
in their lives that it surprised her to realize how
desperately she wished happiness for them. Oh,
she knew it would always be a blemished happiness now. Nothing would erase the abuse they'd
suffered or the scars that abuse had caused. But
Katrina was young enough to outgrow it, given the
opportunity. And Leesha was bright enough and
determined enough to work through her misery
and take control of her own life the way—Janet almost flinched. The way I took control of mine, she
thought. Leesha reminds me of me.

It was a disconcerting idea, one she did not appreciate. But Janet took great pride in her ability

to face reality, even when it was not a reality she cherished. She had fought hard to escape her mother's attempts to convince her that all truth is subjective, that one need only imagine reality to make it so. Sometimes she regretted that she could not subscribe to some such comforting theory.

Soothing philosophy and platitudes would be particularly welcome now, she thought as she watched Leesha struggle with her breakfast. Nothing would make her happier at this moment than to believe that Melinda Forrest would be found innocent and set free to be with her children.

In fact, Janet felt certain that Melinda would be found guilty of the murder of her husband. How could a jury ignore the facts? And how could a jury be expected to acquit her when even Janet and Sarah Elizabeth believed she was guilty?

"Call the police," Eliza said.

Sarah Elizabeth, struggling to dress herself and eat breakfast at the same time, did not react with her usual alarm. "Why?" she asked, hopping around on one foot while she tried to put a shoe on the other.

"There is a hobo lurking about the estate," Eliza explained.

Janet looked up from her third cup of coffee, mystified.

"We don't have an estate," Sarah Elizabeth said calmly. "We have a half acre."

Ignoring dimensions, Eliza repeated herself. "Call the police. I'd do it myself, but you have a better understanding of the procedure than I." It did not sound as if Eliza admired this knowledge.

"How many hobos did you see?" Sarah Elizabeth asked, and popped the last bite of pastry into her mouth.

"One. Isn't that sufficient?"

"Mother Eliza, I doubt we have even one hobo in Jesus Creek these days. I believe they've all been relocated to the old hobos' home, out west somewhere."

"Your attitude is quite unacceptable," Eliza warned her. "Would you have those filthy people invading our home while we sleep? I can't bear to imagine what they might do to us."

"It's Henry Mooten, if you've seen anything at all," Sarah Elizabeth explained. "I've hired him to guard the property so we can all sleep better."

Sarah Elizabeth had not stretched the truth too far, Janet conceded. *She* felt safer knowing that Henry was on the job.

"Henry Mooten!" Eliza was more upset now than she had been thinking that hobos were setting up camp in her backyard. "That man is a lunatic. His entire family, for as far back as I can remember, has exhibited queer behavior. His grandfather was a most peculiar man, partial to preaching in the street."

"On the subject of lunacy, I defer to your expertise," Sarah Elizabeth snapped.

Janet had noticed that Sarah Elizabeth had grown increasingly impatient with her mother-in-law of late. Not that this was difficult to understand, but it was out of character for the usually mild-mannered Sarah Elizabeth.

More stress, Janet surmised. Put her in a locked room with Mary Ann and their combined stress level would hit critical mass. They could blow a hole through the earth that would suck them and everyone around them into it.

Where in the Nanny Cares program, she asked herself, does it say that I have to baby-sit the adults? It wasn't the only item of importance that Nanny Cares had failed to address, as she was learning every day.

"I will keep a close watch on the property," Janet said quickly. "Should I notice unauthorized persons wandering about, I will without hesitation contact the authorities."

"Thank you," Eliza said stiffly, not happy to be indebted to Janet. To Sarah Elizabeth she whispered, "The servants are taking over your place in this house. Perhaps they should." Then she stalked out of the kitchen, happy with the injury inflicted.

"Fine with me," Sarah Elizabeth called after her.

Closing her eyes and drawing in a deep breath calmed her somewhat. "Sorry, Janet. Everything she does gets under my skin these days. I don't know what's wrong with me."

Janet could have explained, but she was thoroughly tired of pointing out to other women that their stress levels were out of control. Her own peace of mind was rapidly eroding, too.

"I'm planning to pay a call on Mary Ann today," she said.

"Good." Sarah Elizabeth, digging frantically through her purse, was clearly uninterested in Janet's plans.

"I'd like to talk to her about what we discussed last night," Janet added, lest Sarah Elizabeth had forgotten why it was important for her to visit the neighbor. She could not bring herself to mention the specific topic she planned to cover.

"Oh, that." Sarah Elizabeth bent to retrieve a pen that had fallen out of her purse during her search. "Have I mentioned lately that I'm sick of battered women? I talk to them, I talk *about* them, I dream about them . . . I'm drowning in damned battered women. I am sick of battered women. And I can't find my keys."

Janet reached across the table and picked up the keys that Sarah Elizabeth had laid down there when she'd first opened her purse.

Sarah Elizabeth snatched them away, as if Janet had been hiding them from her. "Thanks," she said without a trace of warmth. She started to leave the room, stopped in the doorway, and said, "Even if she is, she won't admit it."

Janet assumed this referred to Mary Ann being a victim of violence. She further assumed that Sarah Elizabeth, jaded and bitter, was wrong. Mary Ann was doubtless afraid of revealing her plight for fear of being ridiculed. Once Janet made it clear that she was there to help, the walls would come down and Mary Ann would gladly take advantage of the opportunity to escape. It only made sense.

Ariel had fallen asleep in Janet's arms as soon as they sat down in Mary Ann's kitchen. Another time Janet would have eased the baby gently into her crib or onto a floor pallet, but with the other two children playing in the room, she feared for Ariel's safety. Besides, Ariel's gentle weight was pleasant and Janet enjoyed reaching down occasionally to touch the little bit of fuzz on her head.

Katrina and little Eddie were building a fort. It had been Katrina's idea and she, being the older of the two, had easily convinced Eddie to go along with the plan.

"First we build the fort," she'd explained to him.

"Fo't," Eddie parroted.

"Right. Then we can put the people in it." Katrina grabbed a Barbie doll she'd dragged along with her and held it up for Eddie to see. "Then *no*-body will be able to get them and hurt them."

It seemed an awkward moment to Janet, but Mary Ann did not react at all, so she shrugged it off.

Mary Ann filled the coffee maker, wiped a few drops of water from the countertop, and carefully hung the dishtowel inside a cabinet door, making

sure the edges lined up exactly. Finally satisfied
that her kitchen was once again in order, she came
back to the table to join Janet. "Ted's so excited
about his boat," she said. "He's like a kid at Christmas. Last night he kept looking out the window at
it."

"I'm not surprised," Janet said. "After all, with
the damage done to your car, it's only natural he'd
worry that the same vandal might return and destroy his boat."

Mary Ann gave her a questioning glance. "I told
you, Janet. It has nothing to do with Ted. It wants
me." She sighed and dropped her head, as if to say
that she was hurt and disappointed by Janet's
words. "You think I'm crazy, too, don't you? Maybe
you're right. Ted says I must be."

"I don't doubt your story at all, Mary Ann. I certainly don't believe that you're insane. But unex-
plained violence aimed at you would not rule out
the possibility that a human hand slashed your
tires."

"I suppose not," Mary Ann said, clearly unconvinced.

"I notice your car is still unrepaired, by the way.
Have you made an appointment to have the tires
replaced?"

Mary Ann rose to check the coffee. "No, not yet.
New tires cost so much. Even retreads are a fortune these days."

Janet did not reply, though she desperately
wanted to point out that new tires cost far less
than a boat, or that a working automobile was
more necessary than a recreational toy.

"I don't miss the car anyway," Mary Ann went
on. "It's not like I go a lot of places. Actually, this
is nice. It gives me a good excuse to stay home. I'm
so tired lately I don't have the energy to be galli-
vanting all over the county. And there's so much to

do around this house. I spend hours and hours cleaning, but it never gets done. There's always another spot on the floor, or another pan to wash."

"Sometimes a change of scenery will improve one's state of mind and make the drudgery of housework less disagreeable," Janet suggested. "A drive through the country. A shopping trip. I haven't taken a trip out of town since I first arrived here. Why don't we plan an excursion for my next day off? You could get a sitter and—"

"Oh, I never leave Eddie with a sitter. These days, you never know what someone's going to do. Terrible people. In fact, I don't believe I've ever left him with anyone who wasn't family, and even then I'm nervous. Eddie is my whole life." She gave Janet a smile dripping with sympathy. "You just can't imagine what it feels like to have your own child. Before Eddie came along, I was so empty. I remember thinking, way back when I was just a child myself, how glad I was to be a girl so I could be a mother someday."

The coffee had finished brewing, and Mary Ann rose to take mugs from the overhead cabinet. "Do you need sugar?" she asked, setting Janet's drink on the table and returning to the counter to pour for herself.

"No, I prefer my coffee black." Actually, Janet thought, I prefer something other than coffee.

"Not that I'd expect other people to go without sitters," Mary Ann went on. "Sarah Elizabeth has you, and anyone can see that you're taking wonderful care of—"

"Mary Ann!" Janet had watched in horror as Mary Ann poured coffee into the mug, and then continued to pour as coffee spilled over the lip and onto the countertop. Even Janet's cry of alarm did not stop her.

Still holding the pot tilted and pouring, Mary Ann calmly asked, "What?"

"Coffee! Coffee!" Janet leaped from her chair and pointed, unable to jump across the dividing bar with Ariel in her arms.

"Oh!" Quickly setting the pot down, Mary Ann grabbed a dishtowel and started dabbing ineffectively at the spill. "I'm so clumsy," she said with a laugh.

"It didn't appear to be clumsiness, but absentmindedness. Mary Ann, I have noticed that you seem a bit distracted lately. Now please, sit down."

"I'm always doing something like that," Mary Ann went on. "You wouldn't believe how many times I've lost my shoes or forgotten to take my car keys to the car or tripped *up* the stairs."

"Sit, please." Janet decided that Mary Ann could well do without another cup of coffee, since it seemed the woman was already jittery enough. "Don't worry about the drinks."

"It's okay," Mary Ann insisted, even as tears rolled down her cheeks. "Let me clean this up and everything will be fine."

"Mary Ann, you can't deny that you are upset. I realize your concern about what may be happening to you is difficult to express. I want you to know that I will do all I can to help you. You can place your trust in me."

Wiping her eyes with a fresh dishtowel, Mary Ann then proceeded to fold that one, edges aligned, on the towel bar. "Oh, now I've got you worried. I didn't mean to stir everybody up so. And I do appreciate your concern, Janet, but I probably am just a little crazy. It's that time of the month, after all, and Ted can tell you how I get. I don't know how he puts up with me."

Janet wasn't at all surprised that Mary Ann refused to admit the truth. Perhaps, as Delia had said, she did not consider herself an abused woman. Realizing that it would not be wise to confront Mary Ann with an accusation, Janet tried to work around the subject. "I've tried to think of all the possible reasons for your problems," she said. "And I assure you, I've taken seriously the possibility that this house is haunted. I don't feel, however, that that is the most likely explanation. I do wish you'd have a medical examination. It would, at the very least, rule out ill health."

"I keep telling you, I'm not sick. I feel great. Just a little tired." The fact that she sat limply in her chair with barely enough energy to swear to her own good health made the statement less than fully convincing.

"If Eddie began to behave strangely, to hear sounds that no one else heard, or if he became pale and listless, wouldn't you insist on taking him to a doctor?"

"Of course. Eddie's my baby, and I've always made sure that he has his checkups and shots. Our pediatrician is one of the best in the South, by the way. I know Sarah Elizabeth just takes Ariel to Dr. Porter here in Jesus Creek, and I'm sure he's very good. I know Sarah Elizabeth tries her best to be a good mother, but she has so many demands on her time. Maybe you could convince her to start taking Ariel to—"

"I was talking about your health, Mary Ann. Not Eddie's or Ariel's."

"My health is just fine." It was a wooden statement, but one Mary Ann obviously intended to stick to.

"Very well, then. We'll move on to other possibilities. For the moment, remember, we are exploring *all* avenues, even those that may seem improbable." Janet watched closely to be sure Mary Ann understood.

"Fine. What else have you thought of?"

"The noises you've heard."

"Voices," Mary Ann corrected her.

"Yes, I realize they sound like voices. But could it be an auditory illusion? The wind, for instance, or the hum of household appliances?"

Mary Ann shook her head, although not so firmly as she might have. "I don't think so. Maybe. I don't know."

"Sometimes cracks in the foundation of a house will produce—"

"That's not likely. Ted inspected the house before he bought it."

Measuring her words, Janet moved on to the topic she'd been waiting to discuss. "Could it be stress?" she asked. "Problems that may not seem worth considering, but that have accumulated and now form a great ball of worry?"

"I can't think of any," Mary Ann said with all sincerity.

"Friction in your marriage?" Janet asked gently.

Mary Ann's mouth dropped open. "Are you kidding?" she asked, genuinely stunned. "Why, Ted's a doll. He's absolutely the perfect husband. He adores Eddie and he's an excellent provider."

"But if he is under unusual pressure. At work, for example. That might cause him to—"

"Even if Ted had trouble at work, which he doesn't, he'd never take it out on me or Eddie. He's the most patient person I've ever met. He'd have to be, wouldn't he?" Mary Ann laughed. "I mean, to put up with me."

"But, if—"

"Janet, you've been spending too much time listening to Sarah Elizabeth talk about those women she works with. You think all men are beasts. But it's just not true. Look at me. Look at this house. Does this look like the home of a wife beater?"

Janet obediently looked around the kitchen, at the ducks on the wall, the neat row of canisters, the carefully measured and perfectly coordinated knickknacks. Everything was there, in its place, performing its appropriate function. Still there was something that Janet's mother would have called *restless* about the room. Janet had never understood it when her mother said it, nor did she understand now when the word came into her head. She was certain, though, that it was more than her own imagination.

"I'm not sure what a wife beater's home *would* look like," she said truthfully.

"Well, not like this. Janet, Ted's got a master's degree in engineering. I've got a bachelor's degree. We're upper-middle-income, well-educated, decent people."

"Yes?" Janet waited for her to make her point.

"For heaven's sake. Look, Janet. Ted has never laid a hand on me. And he'd better not. I just wouldn't put up with that, and I'd think you'd know it." Mary Ann was at last animated. She sat straighter in her chair and was breathing as hard as if she'd just gone a round with Sugar Ray.

"I only meant to suggest that *if* you and Ted were spatting, it could have caused emotional stress. Enough, perhaps, to cause depression and anxiety."

Mary Ann rose from her chair and began pacing again. Her agitation was no greater than it had been when Janet first arrived, but it was more clearly focused. "I don't want to talk about this anymore. Why, Ted would be furious if he thought you suspected him of hitting me. He thinks those men are just awful. Ask him. He'll tell you there's no excuse for it."

Janet found Mary Ann's denial of abuse convincing. The poor woman was stunned and outraged that she had even hinted at such. And certainly, it was a relief. She had not wanted to believe it and was more than willing, now that she'd gotten Mary Ann's reaction, to forget her suspicions.

She had been impressed by Ted's thoughtfulness and by Mary Ann's obvious love for her husband. It was a marriage to emulate, Janet had thought, and was glad to know that she still could.

"I'm glad," Janet said, and she was. "I hope you understand why I had to ask. If you were being victimized, and I'd done nothing to help, I could never have forgiven myself."

Mary Ann flashed a quick, forgiving smile. "It's good to know I have a neighbor who cares," she said lightly.

"We must get back now," Janet told her, feeling that the time was right to let some breathing space into their friendship. "Come along, Katrina. Bring your doll."

"Don't forget the keys," Katrina said, clutching her Barbie to her chest.

"I never forget keys," Janet told her. "If you don't mind, Mary Ann, I'd like to plan an excursion for us. I understand that you don't want to shop, but please let me work up something."

"Leesha did," Katrina told her doll, and led the way to the kitchen door.

"Okay, then." Mary Ann gave in gracefully. "You plan it, and let me know when. I'll talk to Ted about it."

Janet left the Thorn home feeling as if she'd won a major victory. It was a relief to know that she no longer had to worry that Mary Ann might be hiding bruises or living in a tormented marriage. But still something tugged at the back of her mind, something that she refused to contemplate because instinct told her that survival sometimes depends on denial.

Glancing back over her shoulder, Janet thought she saw Mary Ann at the back door, staring blankly across the yard. The gray sky cast a shadowy haze that made it impossible to be sure that what she'd seen was in fact Mary Ann. It might have been a shadow, or a reflection on the glass. In a fanciful moment, Janet thought it could have been a half-invisible ghost.

She stopped, one foot on the bottom step of the Leach porch. That was exactly it, she realized. Day by day, Mary Ann had been disappearing.

Janet's mind would not be still. She had tried reasoning with herself. She had tried warm milk. Worst of all, she had tried her mother's favorite remedy, meditation.

At last she wound up in a chair by her bedroom window, reluctantly watching the house next door. From where she sat, she could not see the backyard and therefore could not be certain that Henry Mooten was on patrol. She hoped he was, and realized just how bad her mental state was. What has it come to, she asked herself, when I feel safer with Henry around?

The afternoon had been full of children, ringing phones, household errands and a thousand other time-filling chores. Janet had not been aware of giving thought to any particular mystery, but apparently her subconscious had continued to grind out questions and answers. Now she was stuck with them.

Earlier, when she'd related her conversation with Mary Ann, Sarah Elizabeth had eyed her cynically and said, "What did you expect her to say?" It was unlike Sarah Elizabeth to be sharp-tongued. Living with Eliza was doing her no good at all.

Unwilling to subject herself to Sarah Elizabeth's ill humor, Janet had not pursued the subject. Instead she had pleaded a headache and cocooned herself in her bedroom long before the household turned in for the night. Isolation had proved a poor choice, she now realized. She would have been a much happier person if she'd stayed downstairs and listened to Eliza criticize Sarah Elizabeth's mothering skills.

Had she thought of it earlier, she could have called Delia Cannon for advice. Too late for that now, she realized. The decision was hers to make, as if there could be any doubt about what that would be.

Come morning, Janet would have to confront a murderer.

CHAPTER

11

ARIEL WAS NORMALLY A SWEET-TEMPERED child, calm and tolerant of minor delays or disruptions in her schedule. Perhaps it was the combined morning chaos of the household that had made her fussy, or perhaps the baby had learned to recognize Friday mornings and knew that her mother would be frazzled and battling the hotline in a few hours. Whatever the cause, Janet could not get Ariel quieted and the constant whining was becoming an almost unbearable nuisance.

She finished dressing the uncooperative baby in a warm sleeper and brushed her fine hair into a peak. Even grumpy, Ariel was adorable, Janet thought.

Down the hall, Leesha was arguing with a stubborn Katrina. The younger girl wanted to dress in a sunsuit and cowboy boots, despite the cool autumn temperatures. Instead of changing her clothes, as Leesha had told her to do, Katrina was amusing herself by digging through the suitcase that served as Leesha's closet, tossing items of apparel about the room the way a tornado tosses trailer parks. It was only one more symptom of Katrina's increasingly disturbing behavior. Had she been an ordinary child, Janet might have taken her to task, even hauled out the big punishment and banished her to her room for the morning. Given the circumstances, she'd decided to give Katrina time to adjust to the stress created by her mother's imprisonment.

Thinking a firm, adult voice might be of use, Janet carried the still-whining Ariel into the girls' room. "Katrina," she said sternly, "stop that this instant. Your sister is trying to dress for school and you are old enough to clean your own mess. Now change your clothes and come down to breakfast."

Katrina ignored her.

"She's being a little brat this morning," Leesha said, running a brush through her hair. "Katrina, put my clothes back. I mean it. I'm not going to clean up after you."

Katrina continued her game, unimpressed by either Leesha's tone or Janet's glare. This is not my job, Janet realized with relief, and turned to go, leaving Leesha to deal with her obnoxious sibling for the time being.

Eliza Leach stood in the hall, dressed entirely in black and looking like a hungry vampire. "This is not acceptable," she said haughtily. "Sarah Elizabeth! Sarah Elizabeth, come out here and explain this."

Sarah Elizabeth's bedroom door was jerked open in response. "What?" she demanded. She was dressed only in a full slip and panty hose, her wet hair combed straight back, and no makeup yet in evidence. "What do you want?"

"Please explain why our morning hours have been assaulted by this din. A well-run household should proceed smoothly and without incident. You must learn to maintain control over the servants.

Someday this house will be yours to run, Sarah Elizabeth. If you don't take the time to learn your job properly now, while I am here to guide you, how do you expect to handle it when you are on your own?"

"Well, whoopee shit," Sarah Elizabeth snapped back. "When it is my house, I might burn the damned old shack and be done with it. As for how I'll run it without you, I thought that's what I'd been doing."

"Sarah Elizabeth, your language," Eliza chided. "We must set an example for the help. 'A servant sees himself through the eyes of his master.' Never forget, Sarah Elizabeth, that our inferiors look to us for guidance."

Ariel, disturbed by the open hostility between Eliza and Sarah Elizabeth, began to cry in earnest. Leesha discreetly closed the bedroom door, but Katrina immediately opened it and poked her head through to follow the action more closely. Janet was perhaps most uncomfortable of all, but could not escape the scene without walking between the feuding women and calling unwanted attention to herself. Nanny Cares had not prepared her for open warfare.

"Look, Mother Eliza. Why don't *you* run the house if you don't like the way I do it? Haul your butt out of that room for a change and do something useful."

"Your tone is not appreciated, my girl," Eliza warned.

"Neither is yours, you old bat," Sarah Elizabeth flung back.

"Really!" Eliza drew herself up, as if preparing for battle. "Lindsay James shall hear of this unbecoming behavior. I trust you will have improved your temper before he returns. It isn't good for a

man's digestion to have his dinner interrupted by a
pouty wife."

For a moment Sarah Elizabeth stared at her
mother-in-law in disbelief. Then, as if she'd been
slapped, she burst into sobs and ran past them all
to the bathroom at the end of the hall, where she
promptly locked herself in.

"In my day," Eliza said to no one in particular,
"young women were raised to respect their elders."
Then she, too, retreated to her room.

Looking like a wholesome teenage girl in jeans
and deep blue sweater, Leesha sat in the floor, eating a piece of toast with one hand. With her other
hand, she held out a strip of bacon to entice the
puppy. It seemed interested, poking first its head,
then the upper portion of its body through the door.
Sniffing the meat with obvious desire, the puppy
moved forward inch by inch until it was able to nib-
ble at the bacon. Given a choice, the dog no doubt
would have snatched the bacon and run back to its
hiding place behind the washer, but Leesha held
tight, thus forcing the puppy to stand beside her
and eat.

Taking care to move slowly, Leesha gently
reached around the dog's body with her arm and
carefully scooped it up. Intent on eating bacon, the
puppy did not object. For the first time since Sarah
Elizabeth had brought it home, the puppy willingly
allowed itself to be touched by a human hand.

With Ariel wiggling in her lap, Janet watched the
amazing scene with awe. Leesha's patience had
earned her the puppy's cautious trust.

Her maturity and no-nonsense attitude led one to
believe that Leesha was an adult. This morning,
though, playing with the puppy, and her hair
pulled back into a ponytail, her fresh, youthful face
reminded Janet that she was a child, full of the im-

pulsiveness that led to action without thought for the consequences.

The girl had qualities that anyone might emulate to advantage—she was kind and conscientious, and intelligent enough to know that she must plan ahead and work hard to achieve the kind of life she wanted for herself. It sickened Janet to think those qualities would be wasted.

"Good job," Janet said quietly. "I had begun to think that animal would never be tamed. It looks as if you've done what none of the rest of us could hope to do."

"Just takes time," Leesha replied. "Some things have to be built up slowly, like making friends and learning to trust. Animals are basically trusting, if you give them a reason."

This comment did not make Janet feel the least bit better about what she must do. Ariel sensed her uneasiness and gave a sharp cry of complaint. Much as she disapproved of her own action, Janet stuck a bottle in the baby's mouth to pacify her.

"Leesha," she said, "we must speak frankly. Tell me about the car keys."

Leesha looked up, gave her full attention to Janet. She did not seemed surprised by the question, and there was no hesitation in her response.

"I was going to the police chief this afternoon," she said. "I wasn't going to let Mom take the blame. Honest."

"I'm sure you intended to tell the truth. No doubt you haven't spoken up before now because you've been frightened."

"Yes," Leesha said. "I'm ashamed of myself for being so scared. I know Mom's a lot more scared than I am, but I just couldn't—"

"No need to explain. However, I must confess that I am extremely concerned about your future.

You must not go into this alone. First we will talk to your mother's attorney."

"About what?" Sarah Elizabeth asked. She finished dressing and her hair was groomed, but her eyes still showed the effect of a good cry and her overall manner was one of miserable exhaustion.

Turning to her employer, Janet explained. "Leesha is going to explain to Chief Gassler that she, not her mother, shot and killed Mr. Forrest."

"Oh, Leesha, honey!" Sarah Elizabeth dashed forward, frightening the puppy, who jumped to the floor and fled back into the laundry room. "Honey, I know you're worried about your mom, but you'll just have to believe that she'll be found innocent."

"She *is* innocent," Leesha reminded her.

"Of course she is. And it's wonderful of you to make this effort, but don't you see? No one's going to believe you anyway. And it will cause more trouble in the long run. Mr. Maddox has everything under control."

"Sarah Elizabeth," Janet said impatiently. "Pay attention to what she's saying."

Pausing only to glance at Janet, Leesha began to speak. Her voice was calm and unemotional as she confessed to killing her stepfather.

"He'd been drunk all afternoon. That always meant trouble, and we knew it. Mom knew it. I tried to get her to leave earlier that day, but she said she had to cook supper. She said James would get even madder if she didn't. And then he got mad anyway. I don't know about what."

Sarah Elizabeth had finally begun to understand how serious the discussion was. She sat down on the floor beside Leesha, hugging the girl to her, unable to speak.

"They were in the kitchen and I heard him start yelling at her. By the time I got in there, he'd already started hitting her. I knew she'd have a black eye. You could see where he'd punched her face. Mom just kept backing up, until she was against the wall. That's happened so many times before I can't tell you. And then he picked up a chair and started swinging it at her. Mom put her arm up, to protect her head, you know. That's when he broke her arm. I heard it, and I knew right away it was broken."

She looked up at Janet. "If it had been her right arm, they might have decided that she couldn't have fired the gun. Being right-handed and all. Do you think?"

"I don't know," Janet answered truthfully. "Probably not."

"Anyway, he was so drunk by then that he lost his balance when the chair came down. So while he was trying to get up and hit her again, I just grabbed Mom's sleeve and pulled her out the door. Katrina was in the living room, and I grabbed her on the way out. I got both of them to the car. I don't know what he was doing. Still trying to stand up, maybe. All this time Mom kept saying how mad he'd be and how we'd better go back in."

Janet had spent a long night thinking through the possible scenarios, including the one she was hearing now. She could see, though, that Sarah Elizabeth was caught between disbelief and shock. Janet would have tried to comfort her if she'd had any idea how to go about that. As it was, she was barely able to hold back her own tears and a powerful urge to insist that Leesha shut up now and forever hold her peace.

"But then," Leesha went on, "when I tried to start the car, I realized the keys weren't in it. I knew Mom had a set in her purse, but it was in the kitchen. Mom was screaming, 'He'll be so mad. He'll kill me.' And I knew he would, too, if he got the chance. So I ran back in the house for the keys.

I don't think I was scared then, just really mad at him for hurting Mom again."

Leesha shrugged at her own heroics, as if she could not believe she'd gone charging into the house alone.

"James was standing in the door between the living room and the kitchen. He was blocking my way, and he said if we didn't all get back in there right that minute, he'd beat the shit out of us all. You know, if Mom had heard that, she'd have gone right back in there and I wouldn't have been able to stop her. She just doesn't understand that he's gonna be mad when he's mad and nothing she does makes any difference."

Sarah Elizabeth hugged Leesha closer and nodded her understanding while tears ran down her face.

"I knew I had to get those keys. We had to get out of there before he came after us. There's a shelf beside the front door, where Mom keeps pictures of Katrina and me. And James keeps the gun there. He said if somebody comes to the door at night, he wants a gun handy. To defend his family." Leesha smiled at the irony. "So I just grabbed it and shot him. It didn't seem like a big deal at the time, just something that needed doing if I was going to get those keys. I had to step over him to get into the kitchen. I was so afraid he'd grab my leg, but he didn't. And then I got the purse and made sure the keys were in it. But I couldn't step over him again. By that time, I *was* scared. So I went out the back door."

"Where's the gun?" Janet asked softly.

"I stuck it in my back pocket—had to sit on it while I was driving, too—and then threw it in the Dumpster behind the Med Center later," Leesha explained. "I didn't want Mom to see it. I figured she'd know what I'd done and make us go back in

the house to help him. But I wanted to get her to
the doctor, and besides, I didn't want to help him.
I wanted him to die. I knew that was the only way
Mom would ever get away from him."

The three of them sat in silence while the full impact of Leesha's confession hit them. It would be
impossible to keep the truth hidden. Without
Leesha's story, Melinda would almost surely be convicted, and none of them could allow that to happen. On the other hand, Leesha would now have to
face the same charges that had been brought
against her mother.

Janet had spent the night wide-awake, trying to
find a solution to the problem that would allow
them to protect both Leesha and her mother. Obviously, there was no such solution.

She's just a child, Janet thought. One instant of
terror, one act of desperation has destroyed her life.

"If I'd known he was still alive, I'd have shot him
again," Leesha said smoothly. "I'm not sorry."

Sarah Elizabeth had called Pamela Satterfield to
say that she would not be coming to work that day.
She did not explain, but Janet had heard her tell
Pamela to "sit on your thumb and cry about it,
then." If Sarah Elizabeth had once been less than
assertive, she no longer was.

Janet watched as Sarah Elizabeth and Leesha
climbed into the car and headed off to the lawyer's
office. Both were being strong and sensible and
brave. Janet wondered if either of them felt as sick
and depressed as she did. Perhaps they hadn't yet
grasped the situation fully, hadn't considered the
very likely possibility that Leesha would be tried as
an adult when the case came to court.

As soon as Katrina and Ariel were fed and
dressed, and after Janet had checked on the condition of Mrs. Leach, she hustled the girls out the

door and across the yard to seek refuge in Mary
Ann's kitchen. The Leach house was too full of negative energy (Good heavens! That sounded like
something her mother would say!) to let them remain there.

There was no need to keep quiet about Leesha's
confession. Within hours, the entire town would
know what had happened. Janet wanted to tell
Mary Ann, to go over the whole story aloud in
hopes of finding a stray thread of hope that she had
previously overlooked.

Mary Ann was finishing the last of her breakfast
dishes when Janet arrived.

"Shh," she warned. "Eddie's still asleep. Here,
Katrina," she said, reaching underneath the sink
and pulling out a basket stuffed full of toys, "you
can sit right over there and play with these."

"I'm afraid we bring unpleasant news," Janet
said, settling Ariel on her knee.

"Do you smell that?" Mary Ann asked, sniffing
the air.

"Bacon?" Janet suggested.

"No, it's something else. Smells like something
rotten. I've looked everywhere, thinking it must be
a dead mouse or something like that. I've scrubbed
and disinfected and I just can't get rid of the smell.
Maybe this will cover it up at least." Mary Ann
opened a package and held up a small ceramic pot
for Janet's inspection. "Isn't this the cutest thing?
It's scented. You light the candle under here, and it
heats the potpourri in the top."

"Lovely," Janet agreed. "As I said, I've brought
bad news. Sarah Elizabeth has just driven Leesha
to the police station. Leesha has confessed to killing her stepfather."

"You've got to be kidding me!" Mary Ann said.
"That girl killed him?"

"To protect her mother from further violence,"

Janet explained. "It seems the list of victims is not limited to James Forrest or Melinda."

"But a teenage girl!" Mary Ann exclaimed. For the first time in days she seemed alive and reachable, shocked back to reality by the atrocity of the crime. "I can't imagine what her mother must be going through."

She reached into the cabinet for a box of matches and struck one to light the candle in her cherished potpourri dish. "I'm surprised she admitted it, though. You wouldn't think people like that would know how to tell the truth, especially when they know they'll get in trouble."

Before Janet could ask what she meant by *people like that*, Mary Ann tossed the still-burning match into the trash can.

"Mary Ann! You'll set us on fire!" Janet cried.

Looking down as if she couldn't understand what she saw there, Mary Ann spotted the trouble and calmly leaned over to blow out the match.

"I just don't know what's gotten into me lately," she said, shaking her head at her own incompetence, but seeming untroubled by what she'd just done. "It's like I'm not all here."

"Well, you won't be here if you keep that up," Janet said.

"I've always been addlepated," Mary Ann explained, as if this were a scientifically proven fact. "Ted says they must have dropped me on my head in the delivery room."

Janet was not interested in Ted's opinion. She had come to Mary Ann for comfort and found it frustrating that she was receiving nothing of the sort. Instead she had to fight back a lecture on self-esteem.

"That smells better," Mary Ann said, once again sniffing the air. "But I've got to find out what's causing that disgusting odor."

"In all the time I've been visiting you," Janet pointed out, "I've smelled nothing but the fragrance of a well-kept house. You're imagining it."

This assessment caused Mary Ann to look up sharply, her eyes darting about as if she'd been trapped by a large and ferocious predator.

"That's not what I meant," Janet said quickly. She was getting rather tired of Mary Ann's touchy attitude, not to mention her complete lack of interest in the truly important points in their conversation. "As I was saying, Leesha has gone to the police to tell her story. I'd like to believe that the law will take into consideration her age and the abuse to which she and her mother were subjected. I have not mentioned this to Sarah Elizabeth, and of course, I've not asked Leesha, but according to SAN literature, a full sixty percent of men who abuse their wives also abuse the children. It would not surprise me to learn that Leesha and Katrina have both been molested by this man."

"Oh." Mary Ann waved away the comment. "I'm tired of these people carrying on about being molested. You'd think everybody in the world was sexually abused during childhood. That's all they ever talk about on TV anymore."

"Perhaps because it's true?" Janet suggested.

"I can't believe that. I've never known anyone who was molested as a child. As an adult, either, for that matter. Ted says they're just looking for attention."

Janet was stuck for a response. She might have pointed out that there were many less painful ways to draw attention to oneself, but Mary Ann had an opinion that didn't seem likely to change just because it didn't match the facts.

Odd, she thought, that a woman who believes she is being terrorized by unseen demonic forces finds it impossible to accept that others may suffer invisible torment, too.

It was nearly dusk when Sarah Elizabeth returned home alone. Taking Ariel in her arms as soon as she came through the door, she then turned and walked immediately back out to the front porch. When Janet dared to check on them a few minutes later, she found Sarah Elizabeth hugging her daughter close, gently rocking back and forth in the porch swing.

"May I join you?" she asked.

Sarah Elizabeth nodded.

Seating herself on the front steps, Janet waited for Sarah Elizabeth to speak first. Across the street the park statue was disappearing into the evening darkness, and an adventurous squirrel circled it cautiously. Except for the day she'd met Delia there, Janet realized, she'd seen no one using the park for any purpose. She wondered if anyone ever did.

Up and down the street, neighbors were coming out to light their jack-o'-lanterns. One or two cars passed and turned into driveways along Primrose Lane. And next door, Ted Thorn was cleaning stray leaves out of his uncovered boat. Mary Ann, holding Eddie, stood expectantly on the back porch, as if waiting for directions.

"I'm putting the hotline on the answering service tonight," Sarah Elizabeth said at last.

Surprising herself, Janet said, "I'll take the calls tonight if you like. If there's an emergency, I can hand it over to a staff member."

Sarah Elizabeth nodded her appreciation. "I'd rather not have it ring. Rather not know anything about women in trouble. Thanks anyway."

"Was it difficult?" Janet asked.

Sarah Elizabeth knew what she meant. "Leesha

was amazing. She told Reb what had happened and went through the whole story, just the way she told it to us. I think *he* was more upset than she was."

"Has Melinda been told?"

"I don't know. They were going to let Leesha see her before—" Sarah Elizabeth shrugged. "Anyway, there was nothing else I could do, so I left. I feel like I've been shot full of holes. So ragged, and tired." Looking down at the top of Ariel's head, she added softly, "I can't handle it anymore."

From next door they heard Ted shout Mary Ann's name, louder than was necessary. Apparently he hadn't realized that she was standing outside, waiting for him to need her.

"James Forrest is dead. Everyone is glad of it," Sarah Elizabeth went on. "But no one's going to take that into account when Leesha goes to trial. It won't matter that she truly feared for her mother's life. Or that she was doing her best to protect three people from a madman."

"You've said Mr. Maddox is an excellent attorney. He'll think of something." It was the first time in Janet's life that she'd deliberately tried to give anyone a false sense of optimism.

"No, he won't," Sarah Elizabeth argued weakly. "This is real life."

"You stupid bitch!" Ted's voice carried across the air and pierced the quiet. "Get over here!"

Janet turned and watched Mary Ann scurry to the side of the boat. Ted was standing up inside, reaching out toward his wife.

"I'm sorry," they heard Mary Ann say.

"Sorry, my ass! Look at that!" Ted shouted. "Your clumsiness has ruined by boat!"

Janet could not make out the scene clearly enough to determine what Ted meant. The boat seemed in fine shape to her, at any rate.

"It's a scratch," Mary Ann protested weakly.

"On my brand-new boat!" Ted pointed out. "Just get out of my sight! Get in the house and stay there."

Had Mary Ann been a naughty child, Janet still would not have found his words justifiable, not to mention his tone of voice. She started to say something about it, but Sarah Elizabeth had already risen from the swing and started inside the house. Janet followed suit and firmly closed the door against the Thorns' argument and all it represented.

Henry Mooten stood guard duty in the backyard. Janet could see him through the laundry-room windows, conscientiously watching the night sky for signs of alien life.

"You need a name," she told the puppy in her arms. The dog buried its nose in her shoulder as if it disagreed.

"It must be a dignified name," Janet went on. "Not cute. And not pretentious. We shall have to think of a name that suits your personality."

Once the puppy had broken past its fear to befriend Leesha, it seemed to have overcome all its neurotic habits. It had spent the day sprawled in the middle of the kitchen floor, undisturbed by the random traffic of the household. When Janet had come into the room just now to make herself a cup of cocoa, the puppy had actually seemed happy to see her and had gladly allowed itself to be cuddled.

"You should be glad my mother is not here," Janet told the dog. "She once brought home a cat she called Earth's Spirit Rising. Of course, after she left, leaving the poor thing in our care, need I tell you, Papaw and I just called it Cat."

The puppy seemed mildly amused, Janet noted, and this encouraged her to continue her rambling. "Mother once brought home a man she called

Steady Eagle. He was skinny and frightfully near-sighted. Behind his back, Papaw and I called him Beady Owl."

She could have gone on with stories of the sort all night, but talking to a dog was not a habit she wanted to develop. That was probably how Henry Mooten had started, she thought.

Unfortunately a day's worth of adrenaline had accumulated and had hit her in a sudden burst just as Sarah Elizabeth and the rest of the household had gone to bed. Janet had paced her room until she worried that the carpet would never be the same, had fought the desire to stand at her window and watch Mary Ann's house for signs of demons, human or otherwise, and had finally given up on sleep altogether.

She returned the puppy to the laundry-room floor and poured a small amount of food into its bowl. Then, armed with a cup of cocoa and determination, she seated herself at the table to reevaluate her diagnosis of Mary Ann's troubles.

Listening to Ted rant and rave about a ding in his boat, and hearing the disrespectful way he'd shouted at his wife, Janet could no longer believe that Mary Ann was *not* a victim of domestic violence. How, she asked herself repeatedly, could Mary Ann take Ted's abusive behavior in stride? Not only denying that it happened, but proclaiming often that he was a model husband?

She'd heard Sarah Elizabeth and the volunteers talk about denial. She understood that it was an integral part of the cycle of violence. Now she must find a way to drag Mary Ann out of her tunnel and into the daylight, no matter how much her friend resisted.

Maybe she would drag Mary Ann all the way down to the police station, to Leesha's cell, and force her to look at the ultimate victim.

CHAPTER

12

"IT'LL BE A MURDER CHARGE," SARAH ELIZ-
abeth said wearily.

She'd decided to go in to work even though it was
Saturday. Having spent the day before with
Leesha, the attorney, and the police, she could not
afford to let another day's work pile up at the library.

Ariel and Katrina were not yet awake, and Eliza
had given no indication that she was even alive, so
only Janet joined her for early-morning coffee.

"I think you're mistaken," Janet said. "Leesha
was protecting her mother, her sister, and herself."

"They were already out of the house. They could
have kept going. Leesha went back inside, picked
up a gun, and used it to kill an unarmed man.
Trust me, it'll be a murder charge."

"Still," Janet reminded her, "the man was
threatening them. If he had been armed, Leesha
would no doubt be dead now."

"I don't think a jury is allowed to consider what
might have happened." Sarah Elizabeth was ab-

sently stirring sugar into her cup, too exhausted from a sleepless night to care about food.

Janet hadn't slept well, either, tormented as she'd been by images of Leesha in prison. But Leesha was not the only concern she had this morning.

Having overheard Ted and Mary Ann last evening, she had spent a good part of the night reviewing what she knew of them. Sorting out impressions and wishful thinking, she had tried to mentally list only those events she'd witnessed herself. Ted had given his wife roses. Take away any preconceived notions and that was still a kind and romantic act.

"Wouldn't you say," she asked Sarah Elizabeth suddenly, "that a gift of roses is an act of love?"

Caught up in her own depressing thoughts, Sarah Elizabeth was caught off guard by the question. "Why?" she asked.

After Janet explained Ted's tender and devoted behavior toward Mary Ann on that one occasion, she went on to describe other instances when he'd seemed cold or even hostile toward his wife. "Mary Ann doesn't have access to their checking account," she pointed out. "She says she can't handle money well. Do you remember the morning after her car was vandalized? She was distraught, but he offered no comfort at all."

"What do you want me to say, Janet? That he's just not an emotional kinda guy? I don't have to tell you what's going on. You're smart enough to figure it out for yourself."

Janet shook her head. "Apparently I'm not. Ted teases her about her absentmindedness, or about her cooking ability. She doesn't seem to mind. I've heard both Mary Ann and Ted condemn domestic violence. Perhaps I'm being influenced by the stories I've heard from you about violent husbands."

Sarah Elizabeth rose and poured her untouched coffee down the sink, rinsing the cup before turning back to Janet.

"You've probably heard them condemn physical abuse. And Mary Ann probably laughs at his insults because she doesn't know what else to do. Psychological abuse is equally horrific, but it's not solid. There aren't any bruises or broken bones. The victims don't know they're victims, and the abusers—well, if the victim doesn't complain, what's the problem? If she does complain, she's being a whiny, touchy, premenstrual wimp."

Gathering her purse, Sarah Elizabeth cast a wistful look toward the ceiling. "Was that Ariel?" she asked hopefully.

"I didn't hear anything," Janet said. "If you'd like, I can bring her by the library later this morning."

Sarah Elizabeth gave her a grateful smile. "That would be nice. Maybe we can all have lunch together." She stopped in the laundry room on her way out the back door to pet the puppy and was gone.

Feeling at loose ends, Janet decided to make pancakes for breakfast. Digging through the cabinets for ingredients, however, could not keep her mind off the Thorns.

If Sarah Elizabeth was right, and the problem next door was not physical but psychological abuse, what could be done to stop it? Could it cause the mysterious incidents that Mary Ann had taken for demon interference?

Why not? she asked herself. Her mother had often talked about the way in which emotional disturbances manifested themselves in physical symptoms. (As a child, Janet never had a sore throat; she held back words that needed saying. She didn't stub her toe accidentally; her subconscious was throwing obstacles in her path. Janet would have been happier had her mother given her a Band-Aid and a kiss, instead of psychoanalysis.)

The voices that called Mary Ann to her attic room might have been her own desire to return to a hobby that represented enjoyment and happiness. Voices calling her out into the night—well, that was easy. It was a summons to freedom. In a dissociative state, Mary Ann might have followed her imaginary voices, might even have expressed her frustration by trying to claw her way through the door that held her captive.

But Mary Ann had not taken well to Janet's questions about marital discord. Imagine trying to tell her she's a victim of psychological abuse and just doesn't know it, Janet thought.

Still half-convinced that she and Sarah Elizabeth were imagining monsters where none existed, Janet made a firm decision. If Mary Ann's life was not endangered by physical abuse (and there was not a shred of evidence to suggest that), then she would mind her own business. Mary Ann might be perfectly happy with her marriage and Janet was not about to tell her she wasn't.

Henry Mooten raised the alarm just after midnight. It was fortunate that he had been alert, otherwise the Thorn house might well have burned to the ground, taking Mary Ann and her family with it.

By the time Janet and Sarah Elizabeth had wrapped themselves in housecoats and slipped into shoes, the fire department was in attendance, blasting water through the back door and broken kitchen windows. The two women stood on the Leach front porch, watching the activity with a sense of disbelief.

"Has somebody put a curse on us?" Sarah Elizabeth asked, watching the flames as they slowly died out.

Janet thought immediately of Eliza, then realized the question was not intended to be taken seriously.

"I used to think this was such a dull town," Sarah Elizabeth went on.

Mary Ann, Eddie clasped to her chest, stood as close to her home as the heat would allow. Ted meanwhile paced from front yard to back, giving unneeded instruction to the fire department and growling when no one heeded his advice.

Once the fire was contained, and the extraneous firemen began gathering up their equipment, Sarah Elizabeth and Janet walked across the yard to offer sympathy. Ted ignored them, still trying to coordinate the salvage of his house. Mary Ann put her head on Janet's shoulder and burst into tears.

"You can't stand here all night," Sarah Elizabeth said at last. "Come over to my house and warm up. We've got a bed for you. Tomorrow you can deal with this."

Mary Ann glanced at Ted, who joined their circle wordlessly, indicating that he, too, was exhausted and ready to be consoled.

Sarah Elizabeth insisted on bringing them into her kitchen for snacks. Surely none of them would sleep tonight anyway. Mary Ann's face was streaked with tears and soot. In spite of all that might have been going through her mind, she still seemed detached from the events around her. Eddie, unimpressed by the excitement now that the flames were gone, dozed in her arms. Only Ted seemed full of nervous energy. He paced the kitchen with heavy, angry steps, pounding his fist against his palm.

"You must have been out of your mind!" he said

to Mary Ann at last. She ducked her head, as if he'd actually taken a swing at her.

The fire department had had no trouble determining the cause of the blaze. It had started with a dishtowel left on the range. One of the burners had been left on low, and after smoldering for an hour or so, the cloth had burst into flame while the Thorns slept. The damage to the house was relatively light, but the thought of what might have been drove Ted to fury.

"I'm sorry," Mary Ann repeated over and over. "I thought I checked. I always check the stove."

"You'd have to be an idiot to leave the stove turned on *and* a dishtowel on top of it. I wouldn't be surprised if you did it on purpose, just so you'd have an excuse to remodel. Again."

"Ted, really. I thought I checked the stove. You know I'm so careful about that."

"You're not competent to take care of yourself, let alone a baby. I may have to send Eddie to my mother's until you get hold of yourself and straighten up." Snatching Eddie from his mother's arms, Ted stormed out the back door and across the yard to his own charred house.

"Ted, stop!" Mary Ann called.

Trying to defuse the situation, Sarah Elizabeth caught her arm as Mary Ann stood to run after her husband. "Let him cool off," she said.

"But he took Eddie," Mary Ann wailed.

"Eddie will be fine with Ted. You're tired anyway. Why not go upstairs and rest while you have the chance?"

Tearing away from Sarah Elizabeth, Mary Ann dashed out the back door, screaming "Eddie! Eddie!" as she raced across the yard in pursuit of her husband.

"Whew!" Sarah Elizabeth said, dropping i

chair. "They're about to have a knockdown, dragout."

"Do you think Mary Ann will be safe? I mean, Ted is extremely angry and—"

"He's upset and probably scared. At most he'll yell at her some more and make her feel like dirt. She's used to that."

Janet thought of sitting down herself, but too much excitement was flowing through her body to let her rest. "Why don't I go over there? To act as a buffer," she suggested.

"You'll be sorry," Sarah Elizabeth warned.

"All the same, I'd feel better if I could keep an eye on Mary Ann." Without waiting for further discouragement from Sarah Elizabeth, Janet left.

Henry Mooten, undeterred by the dozens of firemen and gawkers roaming the area, kept a steady watch on the skies. Janet wished him a good evening and kept walking across the yard. Even from the Leach house, she could hear Ted and Mary Ann shouting, but she could not make out the words. Not that it mattered. She could guess what was being said.

As she stepped into the water-soaked driveway beside the Thorn house, Ted came out the blackened doorway, touched his foot to the top step, then tumbled off the porch and sprawled on the ground.

Janet was paralyzed for a moment only, but in that instant Mary Ann came running out the door. She held Eddie close to her body with one arm. Her free arm was raised, and as soon as she had cleared the steps, she flung herself on top of Ted and plunged a butcher knife into his back.

By the time Janet and several of the men who'd been milling about had pinned Mary Ann to the ground and removed the knife from her hand, Ted Thorn was unquestionably dead.

Struggling to be free, Mary Ann turned toward

Ted's body and pleaded with him. "Don't take my baby! For God's sake, don't take him away from me! I'll die, I'll die, I'll die."

October 26

Dear Papaw,

I suppose my last letter was totally incoherent. At that time Mary Ann was still sedated and none of us had any idea what to expect. Since then she has been examined by a stream of specialists and has already begun counseling. When Sarah Elizabeth and I visited her yesterday, Mary Ann kept asking us to keep an eye on Ted. She worries that he will not eat well, since she says he can't cook at all.

The psychologist told us it isn't unusual for a woman who has killed her abuser to be unconvinced that he is dead. After all, he has been the most powerful force in her life, knowing everything she does, directing her movement and her thoughts. He has been God. I fear that her total recovery from this tragic turn of events is as unlikely to happen as Henry Mooten making contact with his aliens.

I'm touched by your concern for me, but I assure you that I am well and continuing to heal. We have returned to the everyday events that keep life on track. This morning I completed a Halloween costume for Ariel to wear—a pumpkin suit, with green-stem hat. I'll be sure to send you a snapshot. You might want to add it to the album that contains photos of all my Halloween costumes, since Ariel, despite my best efforts to remain detached, has become part of my family and therefore of yours.

Mother writes that she has found Bliss, which

probably means (if past experience is an indicator) that she has involved herself in yet another ill-fated romance. Be warned: she is threatening to visit you soon. You've always talked of traveling across the country. May I suggest that the sooner you pack, the better?

I am enclosing a bumper sticker for you to display when traveling through the Southern states. It is a popular one here in Jesus Creek, at least, and I suppose throughout the area. You'll note that it reads: LIBERTY AND JUSTICE FOR Y'ALL. Do not make the grievous mistake that so many outsiders make—*y'all* is a plural *you*. Addressing a single individual in this manner could well get you tarred and feathered.

Ariel has just summoned me with a hearty yowl. This afternoon we are joining Delia Cannon for an old-fashioned candy cooking, in preparation for Halloween. I wonder if Ariel is old enough to lick the spoon.

Love,
Janet

Sarah Elizabeth had refused to let the cool air and scattered showers stop their Halloween fun. Not only was Ariel decked out in costume, but Sarah Elizabeth herself had donned a Wal-Mart witch's cape and hat, while Janet, in a moment of frightening whimsy, had disguised herself as a pirate.

And since it was impossible for Ariel to gum all the candy they collected, Janet and Sarah Elizabeth had been dipping into the bag all evening as they made their rounds in Jesus Creek.

Returning home in the dark of a starless night, giddy from chocolate and their own silly behavior, they were at first confused when Henry Mooten shouted to them to "Look! Up there!"

But following his raised arm, both women were able to make out the bright lights that adorned a dark, cigar-shaped vessel hovering over the Leach house.

DOMESTIC VIOLENCE
occurs in one in every four homes.

Women from every walk of life get beaten. Violence does not discriminate.

A woman may stay with a batterer because she has no place to go, no money, or because she loves him and keeps hoping he'll change.

With time, the battering gets worse and the cycle of violence is passed from one generation to the next.

If you are a victim of battering, you have the right to know that . . .

It is not your fault.
Things can be different.
You deserve something better.

For more information about domestic violence, contact the Department of Human Services nearest you.